Ephemeral Summer

Sheila Myers

ISBN-13:978-1493502714
ISBN-10: 1493502719

Mary —
I hope you enjoy
reading this book as
much as I enjoyed
writing it!

Sheila Myers

DEDICATION

To all scientists who study things, both big and small:
who ford the streams, troll the lakes, and climb the mountains
because they care, deeply.

CONTENTS

PRELUDE

With their rudder-like tails stiffly extended they drop downward in swift descents of thirty feet and more and then bound upward with the lightness of springing thistledown. — Ann Haven Morgan

I watched the mayflies perform their courtship dance above the water as I half listened to the young man standing next to me lament about his shoes.

"I can't understand why they would throw such a fit about my work boots; I mean I have Timberlands on and the guy looks at me and says, you plan to work in those? Go home and buy a real pair of construction boots."

I looked away from the courting mayflies and down at his boots. They were brand new, not a speck of dirt on them. He had done no construction work that day, just paperwork in the office. He was, after all, the developer's son. It was not as if anyone could fire him.

I can't remember his name. His father was developing a dilapidated old mansion located about ten miles down on the east side of the lake. It once belonged to a turn-of-the century millionaire and had been rotting for years. Christened "the Chateau" it was going to be a multi-unit condominium complex and this young man was living in one of the units while they were under construction. Taking a job on one of his father's construction sites must have been a big step. He would be getting to know the business from the ground up. Unfortunately, no one, including his father, had informed him that he would need steel-toed work boots, the root of his irritation.

I turned my attention back to the mayflies. It was dusk and they were very active, swooping in the air, clinging to each other. I could see the females dip down lightly to touch the water, and cause slight ripples; it looked like a soft rain was falling. They were laying their eggs.

"Let's get out of here," the young man said, clearly irritated by the mayflies dancing all around us, landing on our shoulders, necks, and arms. He swiped one off his neck. "These things are biting."

I planted my bike against a tree on the dirt driveway and followed him into the Chateau. What I did not know then, and would have told him if I had, was that mayflies don't bite in their last stage of incomplete metamorphosis because they have no mouth-parts. Their brief existence at this stage is simply to procreate and bring forth life. And then they die.

- Part One Canandaigua -

CHAPTER 1

Water insects and water plants have several points in common. Both groups are very limited when compared with the number of terrestrial relatives and neither of them to any extent inhabits deep water nor lives far from shore. — Ann Haven Morgan

My life might be considered uneventful if it wasn't for the fact that my father killed my mother and then himself when I was fifteen years old. I was not around when this happened, by chance, design, or maybe destiny, I was visiting my Aunt Audrey at the Rawlings' family summer home on Canandaigua Lake. People kindly told me that there was an accident, and that neither of my parents was coming back. Later, I pieced together information from my friends and newspaper accounts. In a twist of irony, my father, Frank Rawlings, who sold pharmaceuticals, was taking anti-depressants, and in an unusual fit of violence, shot my mother, Betsy. Frank Rawlings was a kind, warm, and sensitive person. It was such a shock to everyone that he did what he did. There was never any indication in his demeanor that he could be violent. If there were warning signs, I was not aware and my mother never talked about it with me. One theory was that maybe my mother came upon him when he was trying to shoot himself, and there was a tussle, the gun went off, killing my mother. An accident. In utter despair, my father put the gun to his head and finished what he had started.

My earliest memory is of my mother, dropping me off at pre-school. I was holding her hand, standing in the doorway of the schoolroom. I could not wait to get in there and experience it all; the bright colors, the plastic kitchen, the books, the other kids. She, on the other hand, was not as excited. I could feel it in her grip; she did not want to let go as much as I wanted to leave. I had absolutely no remorse about leaving her, and to this day I feel a bit guilty about that. I wish somehow I could go back and tell her that it was nothing personal, really, I did love her.

My mother was an only child, so after my parents' death I was sent to live with my Aunt Audrey, my father's only sister, in Rochester. She lived in a leafy suburb where the schools were good and the problems facing the teenage youth in 1995 tended to be who was going with whom to the prom, who made the varsity soccer team and who was taking drugs.

My father was 55 when he killed himself, and Audrey was ten years his senior. It could have been trying to live with a 65-year old woman in my teen years but Audrey was not intrusive and did not ask too much about what I was doing or where I was going. I never betrayed her trust in me either. We seemed to enjoy a secret pact: don't mess with my life and I won't mess with yours. She had been widowed three years after her marriage to a college sweetheart. He died in a car accident. She never had children, and by the time I came into her life she was retired from teaching English at the local community college. She spent her time sailing, gardening, or "visiting" with her long-time friend Karl.

Audrey and Karl had an untraditional relationship. Karl

would often come by the lake house and stay for days. He lived and worked in Philadelphia, but had a small camp at the southern end of the lake that I never visited. He was a real estate developer, which kept him busy and away from Audrey for most of the year, but in the summertime he was at his camp and frequently came to see her.

They had known each other since they were young — Karl's family had a camp just a few doors down from the Rawlings. While Karl was in college his father had to sell it to pay tuition bills. Karl was very bitter about that. His family camp had been resold and was now one of the mega-houses that he seemed to hate. The owners were from Florida and only came for a couple of months in the summer, even though it was built as a year-round house, with heat, manicured lawn and all of the other suburban qualities one would expect or want from a house.

The idea that someone would own a year-round house on the lake and only use it for a couple of months out of the year put Karl over the edge. He would get into tirades about the degradation of the lake and the increasing pressure to sell the old family camps because the tax burden of owning lakefront property was getting to be too much for families of modest means. He blamed it all on the big houses that were springing up causing everyone's tax assessments to go up. He would also go on rants about development projects on the waterfront.

Development pressures on the lakefront had started in the 1980s, around the time that the amusement park located on the north end of the lake was sold off and dismantled. Audrey and Karl told me nostalgic stories of the park.

"We would spend days and nights on the rides. The best was the sky ride that went out over part of the lake," Audrey said.

"The amusement park had been around since 1925. Families with young children, teenagers, and college students home for the summer would pull up to the park by boat and make a day of it," Karl contributed.

"I remember we would sit on our porch and listen to the sounds of carnival rides echoing over the water."

It sounded romantic, but the park was sold to private developers and turned into a multipurpose complex of condos, retail shops and restaurants, a decade before I started living with Audrey. I had never known it to be anything else in my lifetime. The rides were disassembled and auctioned off. The original carousel, built in 1909 by a Philadelphia company, was sold to a business that spent a million dollars to refurbish it and have it resurrected at a shopping mall in Syracuse.

What Karl and Audrey missed, what they longed for, was a time, a place, an experience, which was never coming back. What I longed for, what I missed, was my mother's laugh, my father's warm embrace. I couldn't comprehend why Karl and Audrey reminisced about their loss, because it paled in comparison to mine.

Besides, it was tiring for me to listen to the relentless discussions about development around the lake when I was too busy trying to figure out their relationship to each other.

They were both evasive about it. Whenever I broached the subject with Audrey she would just shrug and tell me "Karl is a dear friend."

My conversations with Karl were a bit more informative. One day Karl showed up at the camp on his motorcycle. It was a weekday. Karl's arrivals at our camp had no consistent timing. He would show up randomly, during the week, on a weekend, during the day, at night. Sometime he would stay for days and share Audrey's room and sometimes he was just there for a brief visit. That day was one of his brief visits. He had a slight limp due to a motorcycle accident when he was in his forties. I was reading a book when I heard the cycle pull up and looked out the back kitchen window that faced the driveway to see Karl stiffly get off his bike. In his late sixties, it took him some effort to drag his one bad leg over the back end of the cycle. I could never figure out why he continued to ride a motorcycle after having an accident. He walked into the kitchen that afternoon asking for Audrey, completely beside himself after coming from a lake association meeting and hearing of the latest plans for the marina development across the lake. Developers from Rochester planned to convert the two hundred feet of lakefront and thirty acres of woodlands and fields to a housing community with a private clubhouse and lake access.

"Karl," I remember asking in an attempt to stop him from unleashing one of his diatribes, "you grew up around here, do you know the owners of the marina?"

"Not anymore: The owners are greedy developers. But I did know the old owners. They would never be doing this."

I knew he was riled up and in a mood to talk. I used it as a chance to get more out of him, where had he come from, what was he doing here.

"So you were friends of the previous owners; did my family know them as well? Were they family friends?"

Karl looked at me quizzically. "Why do you ask?"

"Oh, I was just wondering if you all hung out together that's all. Did your family and my family hang out together? Were you all good friends?"

"Yes, I know the previous owners pretty well. When I came up on weekends with my family I used to spend time with the owners' sons, the Lowells, and yes, my parents and your grandparents were friends as well. Audrey and I spent many summers sailing on this lake together."

"When did you meet Aunt Audrey?"

"Oh, I don't know maybe fifty-five years ago or so."

Fifty-five years, and they never married? That is what I wanted to ask next but Karl remembered why he came to begin with, grabbed a can of Coke and asked where Audrey was.

"She's down at the lakefront." I pointed out the bay window overlooking the water. "She was going out on the sunfish."

Karl abruptly left the kitchen and headed down to the waterfront. Audrey was dragging the small sailboat she favored towards the water's edge when she looked up and saw him coming towards her. She waved and smiled. He met up with her and they embraced. Karl began talking and pointing toward the marina across the lake.

I had a lot in common with Karl, although I did not realize it at the time. Like him, I never really understood what drew me to the lake; was it my love of the place or the relationships I cultivated there? This is a question I have yet to answer. What I do know is this: my story ends with my return to the lake after years of being away. But it began that summer when I first discovered the courtship of the mayflies.

CHAPTER TWO

Nearly 500 species of mayfly are known from the United States. Unlike the adult (stage) the nymphal stages constitute a relatively long period in the life history. Most species have an annual life cycle, although a few live two and possibly three years. —
Robert W. Pennak

Audrey did not provide a moral compass when it came to love and relationships. Or at least I thought so at the time, as I watched her relationship with Karl in confusion. And by the time she inherited me, she had always been childless and was nearing a point in her life where providing guidance to a teenager was not in her repertoire. She was a retired teacher, she had her garden, her lake house and friends, her causes, and her own philosophy on life that was unwavering. What she lacked were the parenting skills I thought I needed at the time to make good decisions. She left that part up to me by using the Socratic method she mastered as a teacher. She would ask me what I thought about my decisions, when it came time to make one.

One such time was on a summer evening at the lake

when I was a junior in high school. I asked her if I could go to a party at the southern end with my neighbor Peter. The parents would not be there, a fact I failed to mention to Audrey. On weekday nights it was fairly common for my friends to have parties while their parents were home working in the city, especially at the southern end, where we could be inconspicuous. These camps were nestled along the sides of cliffs and they were, for the most part, seasonal. Families came down on the weekends and stayed once or twice a summer for week-long vacations. The rest of the time the camps remained vacant or were rented by outsiders.

When I asked Audrey whether I could go to the party her response was, "Will you be placed in situations at this party that will make you uncomfortable?"

What was that supposed to mean? Let me see, there would be drinking, smoking pot and cigarettes, loud music, a bonfire by the lake, some kids heading off into the woods to have sex.

"I doubt it," I answered, looking away as I said it. I was not sure which was better, lying about the events that would occur at the party, or disregarding the appropriate evaluation of what was or was not good for me.

"Then go," was her response. It was too easy. Most parents would have asked questions like, 'Will there be adults present?' 'Who is having the party?' 'Where do they live?' This was before everyone had cell phones, and besides the reception at the end of the lake was not all that good, so another question logically would have been, 'What is the number at the camp? I may call to check-up.' But none of these concerns came out of her mouth. And she never worried when I was with Peter. He was a neighbor who had been hanging around the camp ever since I arrived a few years back. Audrey knew his family and trusted Peter.

Peter and I were close. His parents were both doctors and

were never around. They came to their camp on weekends when they could, but Peter, being an only child, was often left alone. He was always an enigma to me and clouded my views on relationships. Because we were so close, I was never sure if our relationship was supposed to evolve into something more than friendship. By my college years I was sexually active, and I placed male friends into two categories: there were the young men I had sex with, because I knew it was not going anywhere and there was no chance of regret but it gave me a temporary feeling of belonging; and then there were the young men I would not have sex with because they were close friends, and I was afraid I would lose their friendship if I took it to the next level.

Peter was in the second category for me. He and I spent a lot of time together talking and taking boat rides. Being an only child allowed him the freedom to pursue whatever he wanted. Peter was an artist, but more than that he was a doer. He was always working on a project. He filled the void of his loneliness through his art, using a canvas or any space he could access. One day I arrived at his camp on my bike to see if he wanted to go into town and get ice cream.

His mother answered the door, “Hello Emalee,” she said, and without further exchange, directed me to the attic.

I climbed the narrow stairs; the attic was a large space, covering the footprint of the house. Peter was hanging an old metal lantern he had found at the dump from a chain onto the rafters above. The whole attic was filled with objects hanging from the rafters; old picture frames, small wooden chairs, plastic wreaths, and paintings he had done. And the items were all interconnected by string making the room look like a spider web of frenzied sculpture. When he saw me enter, he sat down, cross-legged in a yoga style he favored, in the middle of the room to watch me admire his work. He followed my eyes while I surveyed the area and all of the hanging objects.

"You never told me about this," I said.

"I know. I've been working on it all summer." He lifted a piece of cloth off the floor and dangled it in front of him to see how the light filtered through. "This space was not being used except to store old junk so I started to add to the collection with things that I found at garage sales and the dump, and then next thing I knew I had to lift it all off the floor to make room to move. This seemed like the best way to create something out of the junk that was piling up."

"That or you could've thrown it away," I said.

I was always amazed by how he thought. It bothered me. He put a lot of time into creating things that had no value to anyone but him. Who has time to take old junk and display it in an attic as if it is art, where no one will ever see it and you can't even sell it? I wanted to say as much but when I looked over at him — his body framed by the light from the window that looked out over the lake, I did not have the heart to criticize. He looked ethereal, sitting there with a smile on his face admiring what he had done.

But that was not Peter's only project. As soon as Peter started one project, he seemed to be thinking about the next. During the years that we remained friends, he converted his family's boathouse into a dwelling where he lived year-round. It had a roof-top garden where he grew vegetables and stored them for the winter. He insulated the house with all types of recycled material wrapped in plastic sheeting. He found an old wood stove and placed it in the house for heat, and he used passive solar techniques to ensure adequate heating over the winter months. He had odd-shaped skylights protruding from the roof and sides of the house so that while you were sitting inside the place, light appeared in all sorts of angles. His bed was in a loft space in the beams. I stayed there quite a few times and the one thing I remember most clearly was the sound of the water lapping against the flooring below. He decorated the house with his artwork, painting the walls, designing sculptures to rest on the beams. The place was his canvas.

He was a painter and would paint on anything. That was really how he made his money, painting houses for the owners of camps at the lake. He had a brisk summer business and then in the winter he would live at his boathouse and spend his time painting and creating.

For the time I knew him, this is what Peter did. I had a high regard for his friendship but I did not have the artist's soul. Deep inside, I could not comprehend why he spent countless hours creating things just to satisfy, for the most part, himself. But he was a steadfast friend, one that I could always count on, and one that I could talk to about everything. He never judged me and I liked it that way.

Audrey did worry about my safety near the water though, because she knew how much I loved to be in it. The lake is a place of accidents. A lake that big can have mercurial moods and can take away life. With such a big surface area, the lake catches the wind and huge waves can form in an instant. I remember one story Audrey told to frighten me into wearing a life jacket whenever I was on a boat. A 20-year-old man left his house around dawn one day in early May to go fishing, but never came back. By that afternoon his friends and parents were in a panic. Boaters went out looking for him and found his upturned canoe. It was guessed that he must have lost control of the boat when a strong wind came sweeping down the lake, capsized, and drowned in the near-freezing waters. It was weeks before his body came floating to the surface. When the water is that cold, a body may stay submerged for several weeks. It is only when the water warms up, and the bacteria begin the process of decay, that the carbon dioxide gas they release brings the body up to the surface.

And then there was a tragic accident at a party on the

lake. It was in late June, around graduation time, and a lot of my high school friends were there. I was asked to go by the boy that had escorted me to prom that year. After the dancing and partying, I was sticky and giddy. As we were walking back to the car we passed by the neighbor's dock. I just had to get in the lake. It seemed so inviting, the water was calm, the air was humid, and I was hot from dancing all night. It made my date nervous to watch me swimming off the dock at such a late time at night, especially because I was drunk. He would not join me in the water and kept pleading for me to get out.

I was ignoring his pleas when I heard it, the sound every lake swimmer would know: it starts as a slight buzzing, and turns into a whining whir. When I am swimming near shore, that sound raises all my senses. There is nothing worse than the feeling that a boat might be barreling toward shore and not see me in the water.

It was that sound I heard, right before the accident. I recognized it, even though I was drunk. The sound made me reach for the surface, for air, for the hand of my date. I crawled onto the dock as he pulled me out of the water. We stood there breathless and watched the accident happen. A big boat was heading right toward the driver of a small Boston Whaler leaving the party. There was a loud crack as the bigger boat hit the Whaler, a screeching sound as it vaulted over the driver, and then a loud boom that echoed over the water when it landed on the other side. Kids were screaming, 'Oh my God that's Jeff, that's Jeff! Call for help!' It was too late for Jeff, the collision caused massive head trauma and killed him instantly.

At the lake there were guys from the surrounding rural towns who worked seasonally at the local restaurants and vineyards. Then there were the guys who came from out of town — Rochester mostly — who spent summers at the camps their families had owned for generations, hoping to make enough money to keep them in beer over the next school year. The young man from the Chateau development was one of a new breed, newcomers to the area, showing up because their parents bought old places and tore them down, replacing them with a large home that they would only use a couple of weekends in the summer. I did notice subtle differences between the young man at the Chateau and friends like Peter. Whereas Peter could maneuver a boat in water, fix anything that went wrong with it and did not care how dirty it looked, newcomers came with new, high-powered boats that always seemed to break down in the middle of the lake. And when they did, these guys did not know what to do except to call for help, even when the trouble was a minor problem that could be easily fixed.

The favorite spot for us to head to on boats was a place along the cliffs where someone had tied a rope to an oak tree that allowed you to swing out over the water and drop. The spot was perfect for boats to tie up together and idle for the day. There was a short ledge along the cliff if you needed to get out and take a pee on land behind an old willow or oak that dotted the shoreline. Because the cliffs were so high no one lived up above. The land was mostly farmland, left undeveloped and undevelopable due to the sheer height of the cliffs.

The water was crystal clear so you could dive in without worrying about hitting your head on an old branch from a fallen tree or a large protruding rock left over from the glaciers. Any chance I had, I was in the water, even daring to be the first in by late May, when other kids sat on the sidelines waiting until the temperatures reached at least seventy degrees Fahrenheit. My favorite time to swim though, has always been when the lake temperature is equal to the air.

There is an old joke where one fish asks another fish how is the water? And the other fish replies, what the hell is water? I know this feeling, when the temperature, just right, makes it so I do not know my own movements in the water. My skin has no sensation to compare with anything outside of its own climate. This must be what a fish feels —not knowing it is in water.

Every once in a while, a newcomer would show up to the rope-swing on a motorboat with lots of people. They would arrive with their music banging on their loud speakers, and get into line with the rest of us in our small, cast-off Starcrafts and old Boston Whalers — fishing boats, salvaged from parents' boathouses to repair and make do. The only electronic devices working on my friends' boats were the starters and the sonar fish-finder. The new-bloods came with booze and made all kinds of noise to let us know they were there. Their college girlfriends, visiting for the weekend, looked like Victoria's Secret models. Their bathing suits left nothing to the imagination and never, ever felt the water, unless in a drunken fit one of them fell in the lake while trying to pee over the side of the boat. Rather, they sat at the bow of the boats, hoping to catch the eye of someone other than the young men they came with.

The summer I turned twenty, the year of the millennial, after my sophomore year of college, I got a job at the Thendara restaurant, a historical lakeside resort that catered to summer tourists. It was my first foray into waitressing, and one of the most stressful jobs I have ever had. On the plus side though, my sex education came from the bartender at Thendara.

I was in the midst of my non-eventful relationship with the young man from the Chateau — whose name still eludes me — when I was first shocked into realizing that maybe I could get pregnant from these extra-curricular affairs, a fact of life that Audrey neglected to cover. I was talking about my sex life with the bartender, when I was informed that maybe I should be more cautious. Her name was Claire, and she is most likely the reason I never had an unwanted pregnancy. Claire made a good bartender because she liked to listen to people. They were grist for her mill; she loved to write and people gave her story ideas.

It was mid-June and the tourists had not arrived for their summer vacations yet, so the bar was slow that afternoon. Claire asked me if I was seeing anyone. I told her about the young man from the Chateau. We had been together a few times over the past couple of weeks but I had not seen him since our last meeting, a dinner at his house that ended up with us having sex. I related to her some aspects of the story. He picked me up by car, I was wearing a sundress I loved, and I could not wait to go out and show it off somewhere.

"Let's go to my place so I can make you dinner," he said.

I was bummed. We got to the Chateau. He made us a pasta dinner and we drank some wine on the deck looking out over the water. We talked and he reached for my hand and then kissed me very intensely. He led me to his bedroom. His bed was a mattress on the floor, as not all of the furniture had arrived yet. The place was rather stark. I remember the sex was hurried, afterwards we finished the wine on the deck and he took me home. I had not heard from him since.

"What were you using to protect yourself?" she asked.

"What do you mean protect myself?"

"I mean birth control."

"Uh" I said awkwardly. This was a bit too intimate. "I think he used a condom."

"What do you use?" she asked pointedly.

I had a feeling she was not going to like my answer. "Nothing." I replied.

"Emalee are you fucking crazy? You need to get some birth control."

The next day she drove me to the nearest clinic. I was glad she did. At the clinic I got a glimpse of life as a young mother. There were women close to my age looking gaunt and overtired, trying to soothe their babies with plastic baby bottles that looked like they contained kool-aid. I immediately signed up for the pill. Though I had not worried about getting pregnant before, now I felt a bit more secure knowing that having sex would not be my downfall.

I got along well with Claire, but she had a knack for pissing people off, and she did not get along with one of the bartenders, Dave. I was always caught in the middle of their disputes. One thing about waitressing is that you take the brunt of everyone's dissatisfaction: the customers, the bartenders, and the cooks. Waitresses are like moving targets for everyone's wrath. Dave would leave Claire with an un-stocked bar and it drove her crazy to come to work and have to spend time refilling the mixer bottles, stocking the beer, and cleaning the glassware. Dave did not restock the bar again one day and Claire decided she'd had it. She decided to give him a taste of his own medicine.

She and I worked together that night and she refused to restock or clean anything afterwards. The next day I had to take the AM shift with Dave and there was a big engagement party at noon. The people at the party started to rev it up around one, asking for drinks, mostly beer and wine but also a few cocktails. I went up to the bar to pick up a couple of beers I had ordered when Dave realized the bar was not stocked. He was mixing a screwdriver, picked up the mixer bottle, and found it empty.

"God dammit!" he said, and flung the bottle where I was standing. It skimmed my head and landed on the wall behind me, splattering what little orange juice was left. The few people standing at the bar glanced my way with a sympathetic look and a hushed whisper of disbelief. I grabbed my beers and ducked out of there.

While running from the bar for safer territory I slammed into him. Stuart. I had not seen him since last summer. It was at the Owly-Out — a townie bar on the edge of the city. A bunch of my friends and I ended up there on my last night at the lake before I went back to college. Aptly named for its loner quality, the Owly-Out was one of the only bars that did not i.d. students because they needed the business. Another plus was the jukebox. It was up-to-date with the latest hits and we liked to play the music and dance. I remembered when I met him. It was a hot summer night; my friends and I were wind-burned and sunburned from being on the lake all day. Stuart was there with a group I had never met before. They all had family camps on the lake, but they were not from Rochester like most of my lake friends. Instead, he was from some suburb in Connecticut. He was talking to my friend Laurel when I walked over to say hi. Before I knew it we were dancing together. We must have both been caught up in the beer and music because we had worked our way outside to escape the heat and found a bench to sit and make-out. He was at least a foot taller and I remember having to reach up to kiss him, finally ending up entirely on his lap. Things were heating up between us when my gaggle of friends practically fell out of the bar doorway into the parking area. Although we had all agreed that Laurel was the designated driver that night, she was obviously in no condition to drive, and my friends proceeded to argue over who was going to get us all home.

Stuart and I listened to the argument, and then he offered to drive. I remember sitting next to him in the front seat of his car, my girlfriends laughing way too loudly in the back, about something that had happened at the bar. I was a bit embarrassed for them, but holding Stuart's hand on the way home was one of the nicest feelings I ever had. As I was getting out of the car he said to me, "Emalee, can we see each other again?" I was not expecting that question.

"I don't think anytime soon," I replied, "I'm heading off to school tomorrow."

"What school?"

"William Smith College," I called back to him as I climbed out of the car, and ran into my house. That was that. I had forgotten all about it but here he was, a year later.

"Well hello again, the girl from William Smith," he said as he looked down at me in my waitressing uniform of black and white, with a smile of recognition. "I didn't know you worked here."

"I just started this summer," I replied. "How are you?"

"Ok I guess. This party is for my sister. She announced her engagement."

"Great." I stood there wondering what to do next.

"So where exactly is William Smith College?" he asked.

"Two lakes over, in Geneva, NY, at the north end of Seneca Lake. You might've heard it called Hobart. It's Hobart and William Smith. The males graduate from Hobart and the females from William Smith, don't ask me why." I looked up at him, I had forgotten what he looked like but then that night came back to me. I remembered his skin. He had great skin. It glowed a bit in the dark. It was clear and a consistent color, and even when he danced he didn't flush. His eyes were a color I could not figure out though.

Although I was in no hurry to get back to the bar anytime soon, I felt a bit awkward standing there in my black and white waitress uniform trying to figure out the color of his eyes. "I gotta go. Someone at your party is probably looking for a drink," I said.

"Yeah, I could use one as a matter of fact," he said in reply.

I took a round of orders and came back to him with a beer.

"What are you doing later?" he asked.

"Nothing." Was he going to ask me out?

"Well I'm not doing anything either, so why don't I pick you up and we can do something together?"

"OK," I heard myself say, so quickly, I blushed

afterwards.

The next night I could not wait to tell Claire about him, but she was having a fit trying to put the bar back together after Dave's shift. If this battle was going to continue it was going to be a long summer for me. It was an early night at the bar for both of us and I was heading home on my bike when I noticed my tire was flat.

I went back into the bar to call Audrey for a ride but Claire offered to take me home in her boat. I put the bike in and clambered aboard. Claire lived in her parents' camp at the southern end of the lake. Her family lived in Vermont and her parents were older and did not come to the lake as much as they used to. She was the youngest of her siblings and the only one who still stayed at the camp in the summers. She had grown up coming to the lake and did not know what else to do. She liked being alone at her camp because she loved to write and this gave her time to think and do her craft. She was planning to get her master's degree at NYU in Creative Writing that fall.

"I'm glad I get to take you home because I want to meet your neighbor," she said.

"Who?" I asked.

"That Peter boy I've heard so much about," she replied. I didn't know that Peter had a reputation.

"Ok, let's see if he's home." We unloaded my bike at the dock of my camp and headed over to Peter's boathouse.

"Hey Peter!" I called. He was outside on the dock having a beer. "I have someone that wants to meet you."

"Come on in," he said.

The three of us spent the night sitting on his dock talking about the plans for his house and the next project he wanted to start. Claire was enraptured. When I got up to leave they barely noticed my going.

"Well, it's late, I will see you guys later," I said.

"Sure, see you at work," Claire replied.

"Bye," Peter said, barely looking at me. For some reason I was perturbed by his lack of attention. It was not like Peter to just wave me off, or neglect to walk me back to my camp and then say goodnight. I left them engrossed in conversation.

As I walked home I thought about the night before and my time with Stuart.

Stuart picked me up after my long day at the restaurant. I was excited to see him but burnt out from the exhausting runs between customers and surly Dave. Stuart was a breath of fresh air that evening. He was wearing a t-shirt that read: *Reality is for people who can't handle drugs.* I climbed into his car and we took off to a favorite spot of the locals, Bare Hill. I had never been there before. Stuart told me all about it.

"The Seneca Indians believed that a giant snake used his tail to sweep the hill bare of trees. Now the state owns the land and keeps part of it mowed as fields. It has a sacred meaning — a meeting place for the Senecas, even today. In the past, the Seneca Indian leaders met at a big boulder called Council Rock on the hill and at the end of summer they would light a fire to recognize the beginning of harvest. The Seneca people would light fires around the lake to form a ring."

I hadn't realized the tradition of lighting fires and flares lakeside on Labor Day was born from a Native American ceremony. We climbed to Council Rock on the path mowed back by the New York State Conservation Department. Along the way we picked cherries from the trees that lined the path and ate them. We also saw remnants of campfires that some of the local hikers had lit. At the rock our sight was obscured by mature cedar, White pine, and maple trees, so we had to navigate through wet soils to a spot he knew where the views of the lake were best.

"What've you been doing so far this summer?" Stuart

asked.

"Just chasing sunsets and watching the mayflies hatch," was my reply. As soon as I said it I was embarrassed. I only said it because Karl had made a remark recently to me as I was on my way out the door and it stuck with me. I was grabbing my bike planning to ride to the spot I had found where I could watch the sunset in solitude and observe the mayflies when Karl said, "Going to catch another sunset are ya?"

"That sounds interesting," Stuart said, clearly amused by my answer. He thought a bit "You know, I always hear anglers talk about mayfly hatches. Just exactly what does that mean?"

I didn't know the answer. For years I listened to my friends who fish talk about the mayfly hatches and how good the fishing was on the lake. I assumed it meant that they were more actively flying this time of year as compared to the rest of the year. I was to learn later in my studies this was actually their adult stage, a time when they're most vulnerable as fish prey. Otherwise, mayflies spend most of their life as aquatic insects under water, breathing through gills, molting periodically to shed their skins and grow, until they reach the adult stage and became airborne over the water.

We finally came to a spot where there was a break in the trees and the path became bedrock. The view was spectacular. We sat down, and Stuart lit up a joint.

"Want some?"

I took a hit. He told me he went to Wesleyan University; that his family lived in Connecticut. In the summers he worked at the marina across from my camp, the one that was under development. He worked on the boats in the marina, fixing them, cleaning them, and helping the owners get them in and out of the water. His family history in the area was rich.

"My family goes way back. The Lowells were farmers for generations on Canandaigua. Over the years, the family has taken less interest in farming, and the land has been sold off, one parcel at a time to help pay for college and family investments. We also once owned the marina across from your place on the lake. My dad and his brothers sold it a few years ago. I was so sorry when that happened. I grew up around boats, love working on them." He took out his frustration by kicking a small rock by his foot. We watched it cascade down the hill. I glanced over at him, trying to decipher his eyes. *What color were they*?

He changed the subject. "What are you studying at college?"

"Biology. What about you?"

"Oh I am into all kinds of subjects really, though I'm almost finished getting my degree in philosophy."

I laughed, "Well there's a useful subject." As soon as I said it, I regretted it. But he was not easily put off.

"Well actually it is a useful subject. It helps me in all kinds of ways to understand people, look at things logically, and critically. You should try reading philosophy sometime and see if you like it."

I remembered taking a required philosophy class my freshman year and not liking it. Just as I could not fathom why Peter spent so much time creating his art, I could not understand why philosophers spent so much time thinking about life. And as for thinking rationally, or with a critical viewpoint, I thought I had that nailed down already. Except for my addiction to watching sunsets, I was pretty well grounded in reality. Losing two parents the way I did would not allow me to indulge in thoughts about the world and all of its problems, I had my own.

"I like this view," Stuart said.

I looked out, and in a haze of marijuana watched the last rays of the sun setting over the lake.

We left Bare Hill and Stuart dropped me back at my camp. When I walked in Audrey was sitting at the kitchen table stuffing envelopes for the lake association. The flyer's headline read: *Stop the Marina Development! Tell the Town NO to the Sewer Systems!* I sat down to help her stuff.

"What is this all about?" I asked.

"These are flyers explaining the newest proposal the town council is considering for the marina development. They want to buy up a piece of land on the other side of the road so they can put in a mini-sewage treatment plant for their housing and clubhouse. We are trying to encourage the council members to vote against any plans they put forward," she said.

"Why do they need a sewage treatment plant? Doesn't the city of Canandaigua have one?"

"Not one the developers can hook up to; it's too far away, and there are too many houses in their plans for a traditional septic. So if they can't hook up to the sewer, and they can't have individual septic systems then the next best thing is for them to develop their own mini-sewage treatment plant," she said.

"What is to stop them, then?"

"Well, for one thing, they need to purchase the piece of land across the road, and then, the town would have to approve the proposal."

"Who owns the land across the road?"

"That has been in the Lowell family for generations. Most of them don't live nearby anymore. When they sold off the marina they hung on to the last twenty acres of land. I'm not sure what they will do, most of them have family camps near the marina already and do not need the property," Audrey explained. "Who were you with tonight?"

I told her about Stuart.

"Oh that must be one of Bob's sons. He was friends with your dad," Audrey said.

I thought of my father, and remembered that Audrey must miss him too.

"Do you miss him Audrey?" I asked her.

"All the time." She patted my hand and looked at me

levelly. "And what about you?"

"What about me?"

"Do you think about your mom and dad often?"

I looked away. "Yes," I whispered.

"And what do you think about mostly?"

"Well, I wonder why, mostly."

"Why what Emalee?"

"Why my father was so sick that he killed himself and my mother. Why no one knew he was so sick. Why no one helped him."

"It's one of life's great tragedies, Emalee, that so many questions go unanswered."

"Hah," I attempted to laugh so that I wouldn't cry.

"Do you have any other memories about your parents? What about their love, caring, and affection?"

My eyes were welling with tears. I didn't answer.

"You need to recognize your feelings Emalee, it is important to acknowledge them and then try to move beyond. It's not good to be too much in your head all of the time."

That night I had a hard time taking Audrey's advice. My mind was in a whirlwind of emotions that kept me from sleeping. Spending time with Stuart put my mind in a buzz. He was not a guy I could categorize just yet. I liked him too much to just hook up with him and forget about it. But he was not like any male friend I ever had. Peter was the only person to compare him to, and although Peter was a dear friend he tended to be self-absorbed, thinking and obsessing over his projects. I found it easy to be Peter's friend, but he never made me think too hard.

And after Audrey's revelation that my father and Stuart's dad were once childhood friends, I could not stop thinking about my father. I recalled many of his golf buddies and friends at the funeral service. I wondered if Stuart's father was one of them. They lined up to talk to me, telling me how sorry they were, his close friends looking apologetic, as if they were the cause of my father's death. They hugged me and told me that all would be well. Their looks said that maybe, if they had known the pain my father was in, they could have done something about it.

I tossed and turned in my bed, my mind a jumble of emotions, often the case when I thought of my father. Questions raced in my mind: what sadness and rage did he feel that drove him, not only to take his own life, but the life of the woman who loved him most, as well? It was all too much for me and I fell asleep, exhausted from the day.

CHAPTER THREE

A Word of Wisdom: Don't fight a fact, deal with it. — Hugh Prather

Named the "Chosen Place" by the Seneca Indians, Canandaigua is one of the eleven Finger Lakes — ancient river valleys that were carved out by glaciers into deep lakes over ten thousand years ago. Sixteen miles long and 250-feet deep, crystal clear in some places, weedy in others, it is an ideal place to spend summers. Before my parents died, I would visit Audrey at the lake, staying for extended visits. However, we lived in another state, my father's job kept him busy, and my mother worked as well, so my father pretty much gave the place over to Audrey to steward.

And steward she was, not only for the camp, but for a way of life that was fast disappearing in the towns around the lake. Audrey was a tireless campaigner for protecting the lake from all kinds of attacks: from development pressure in the north to irresponsible forest clearing in the southern hills. She was relentless too. She alienated some of our neighbors when she told them that spraying the lawn with weed killer contaminated the lake with carcinogens that 'will kill us all one day' — the lake being her source of drinking water.

In Audrey's youth, people plunked pipes right into the lake and drank their water without a thought of treatment to kill the myriad of bacteria and protozoans that were present. I even overheard one of her sailor friends remark that he used to bring a tin cup on his sailboat and throughout the day just dip it in the lake for a quick drink. Maybe it was cleaner then, but I am not so sure. In her times, the northern end was mostly farmland and the same chemicals and bacteria would probably have entered the water after a heavy rain as it would from the chemically enhanced turfgrass that sprang up in its place.

The Finger Lakes were always a place for people in the region to escape to, to get away from the city life. The first white settlers were pioneers to the region taking advantage of the waterways that connected the sparsely populated villages springing up along the old Native American trails. Rochester was one such city to the West, Syracuse to the East. Once the Erie Canal was completed, the populations in these cities flourished.

The Rawlings camp was a relic, a place still planted in time. My great-grandfather built the camp in 1925 — a rustic outpost for my family to escape the city-life of Rochester. It was built to be a summer camp, located on level land on the east side of the lake, rare in the Finger Lakes except in the north. The camp had four bedrooms, a dining room, family area, and small kitchen, it was not insulated nor did it have a working fireplace. My grandfather wisely bought four acres of farmland abutting his property, which is now forest. The property has the advantage of being situated only six miles from the City of Canandaigua and has always been considered valuable real estate. Because of the prime location and setting, local real estate agents were always approaching Audrey to sell.

On the wall of the camp is a framed note from the

original construction bill. Addressed to my great-grandfather, Harper Rawlings, it neatly lists all of the expenditures for building the camp. Listed on the note are the costs of the nails, the wooden beams, the siding, the roof shingles, the foundation joists, and the slate slabs that grace the screened-in porch. All totaled: $3,550.00. The cost of labor back then was $1.15/hour. The only change Audrey had made to the place since 1925 was to paint the inside walls a white-wash, because she said, the camp was too dark. She did this soon after I came to live with her.

There were the people that had grown up in Canandaigua, and there were summer visitors. For the most part, everyone got along. But there was always a tension because the summer visitors tended to be more urban than rural, and had more money. This became more obvious as people from New Jersey, New York City and even as far away as Florida started to buy up old summer camps and build big houses. Around the time I headed off to college, a grocery chain from Rochester opened up a huge store in the city of Canandaigua, and a Walmart and Lowes were constructed. Canandaigua began catering to various urban tastes for food and drink.

The neighbors also changed the way the lakefront looked, clearing trees from the water's edge for better views and hiring landscapers to plant and maintain hillside gardens in order to control erosion. Places at the southern end, once undevelopable due to steep slopes and lack of soil for septic fields, became ripe for construction as a result of new engineering techniques and sewage treatment technologies.

CHAPTER FOUR

When a (mayfly) brood is at its height, it is a very common occurrence to find piles of the insects three feet square and six to eight inches deep under electric lights. At a neighboring amusement resort several carts were required each morning to haul away the dead insects. —
Dr. F.H. Krecker

I was sweeping dead mayflies off our front porch steps and screens when Peter and Claire arrived by boat to ask if I wanted to hang out at the rope swing. Earlier that day I waded in to wash my hair and only made it up to my knees before the chill took over. The water was still cold even though we were only a few days away from the Fourth of July. I pushed aside the dead mayflies floating in clumps on top of the water, spent from laying their eggs the night before, then dunked my soapy head in, scrubbed it quickly, and rinsed it before my legs went numb with the cold.

Most of the Finger Lakes, Canandaigua included, are large bodies of water that hold their temperature longer than the air. This is a great advantage for farmers that grow fruit of any kind and one of many reasons vineyards do so well around the lake. While the air is warming up in the spring, land around the lake stays cool; the lake moderates the temperature by giving off the cold air it has trapped all winter, keeping the buds from forming too early, or blooming before a killing frost. And in the fall, the reverse happens. As the air temperatures drop on autumn nights, the lake gives off heat, keeping the land around the lake warm and extending the growing season.

For centuries, inhabitants of this region have known about this gift from the lakes. At one time, Seneca and Cayuga Indian villages dotted the landscape, and vast acres of land were planted with crops, including orchards of many varieties. Diaries of soldiers sent to the region during the Revolutionary War to destroy the villages and make way for settlers, attest to this. They describe vast acres of crops, which were burnt to the ground; fruit trees cut or girdled and laid to waste so that the Native Americans would starve or move out. These revolutionary soldiers came back later to reclaim the land as their own; payment for their service to the Colonies during the war. And that is how the area was settled. Today there are many vineyards, especially at the southern end, that make wines and cater to tourists.

I jumped in the boat with Peter and Claire and we took off for the rope swing. Along the way Peter took us to one of the last remaining big boat houses on the lakefront. Used at one time for over-wintering steamboats that cruised the lake from the mid 1800s to 1915, the boathouse was now abandoned. But in its heyday, steamboats carried freight such as fruit, and people, around the lake and eventually to the railroad cars waiting at the Canandaigua city pier. There were over sixty stops along the lakeshore at various vineyards and orchards. Cottagers looking for a ride to the city of Canandaigua would wave a flag to catch the attention of the boat captains and pay 25 cents for the lift.

The old boathouse stood nestled in a cliff along the east side of the lake, just before our spot by the rope swing. Peter killed the engine as we drifted into one of the open bays — the door to the bay had rotted years before.

The mammoth structure extended out on the water and had four boat slips — each one hundred feet long. The ceiling was steeply pitched at sixty-five feet. The three remaining bay doors towered above the water. We got out of the boat to explore. It was a favorite haunt of the kids. I was surprised it had not burnt to the ground by now, given the remains left behind from the recreational activities that went on in there. The neighbors did try to patrol the place, and there was a group trying to raise the funds to renovate it and turn it into a museum for old steamboats. Peter had other plans, as usual. As we climbed along the floorboards, he told us how he thought the place would make a great art gallery.

"I would put in three tiers, lofts that would be open to the floors below so that you could see all of the artwork along the walls. In the center of the lofts there would be a great hole, and a sculpture rising the whole length, from floor to ceiling," he explained.

"Where would you get the money to do all that?" I asked. He looked at me blankly.

"I think it's a great idea," said Claire. "I imagine people could pull up by boat, there would have to be docks next to the boathouse, and they could also come by land and park up above along the cliff."

I didn't see it. I just couldn't imagine people coming to see artwork in an old boathouse, and even if they would, I did not see how Peter could make it happen, not by himself, although now he had Claire on his side. The two of them climbed the ladder to the upper loft as I stayed behind sitting by the boat kicking my feet in the cold water. It bothered me that Claire just went along with all of Peter's lofty ideas. Someone needed to bring him back to reality.

By the time we got to the rope swing I was getting sick of

the two of them, so when I spotted Laurel in a boat nearby, I forgot about the cold water, jumped in, and swam over to join her and my other high school friends. Boy that water was cold. I would bet it was no more than sixty-five degrees, though by the end of the summer it would warm up at least ten more. Even strong swimmers like me are affected by the cold water. I have learned that if I allow my body to relax, and take control of my breathing and swimming, I can manage to swim in cold water, even if it's uncomfortable. But the worst thing that can happen to a person swimming in cold water is hypothermia.

I swam over to Laurel's boat and hung out there for a while. The sun was warm that day and it felt good to bask in the heat after the shock of cold water. As we were laughing about something, Laurel looked up and noticed a guy jumping from another boat into the water.

"Hey, isn't that the guy you made out with last year at the Owly-Out?"

I looked over, there was Stuart, swimming to shore. I could tell he was a strong swimmer. "Yeah, that's him. He and I met up the other night and hiked up to Bare Hill to watch the sunset."

"Really? Well go over and talk to him then, what are you waiting for?"

Feeling modest, I borrowed a pair of her swim shorts to put on over my bathing suit, and jumped in the cold water again, heading towards the spot Stuart was aiming for when he jumped in. As I approached the beach, he was turning around to head back to his boat.

"Hey there," I said.

He looked surprised to see me. "Oh hey, it's you," he said, "what brings you here?" I looked around for an out; I could not let him know I swam to shore just to see him, it suddenly seemed too awkward.

"I am looking for sea glass," I replied.

He smirked. "Sea glass? How cute."

Cute, great, he thought of me as cute. And juvenile.

"Well," I said somewhat defensively, "I collect it for my Aunt. She uses it."

This was true. For years now Audrey had been collecting various pieces of glass that wash up to shore, the broken edges smoothed down by the relentless current. These discarded pieces of beer bottles, old medicine bottles and pottery, come in all shapes and sizes. For as long as I can remember, Audrey and I would spend summers collecting and admiring the pieces we found hidden amongst the black shale, especially the blue ones. Audrey used them to make all types of crafts. She would glue-gun the pieces to old frames, grapevine wreaths, and mirrors and give them away as gifts.

Stuart checked his attitude. "I like to look for it too, I just haven't done it since I was a kid." He changed his tone quickly, "I always liked finding the green glass. It seems like it should be more common, but really it isn't. And the clear is hard to find." We both started scouring the shale for glass. "I always wondered why they call it sea glass anyway; this is not the sea," he mused.

"Maybe they should call it lake glass then," I said. We talked about the glass as we looked for as many pieces as fit in my shorts. I told him about Peter and Claire and our stop at the old boathouse. I told him about my frustration with Peter's plans.

"I just don't see it the way Peter does. He is always like that though, making these grand plans without any thought as to how to execute them. That boathouse needs major renovation and it would cost a fortune to do what he plans to do with it. And he doesn't have any money, and I don't see him getting it either," I told Stuart. "Besides, who would come to a boathouse to see an art exhibit?"

"Probably the same type of people that would go to a boathouse to look at antique boats," he replied. "You'd be amazed at what tourists will do for fun. I'd like to meet Peter sometime. And I wouldn't get so frustrated with him either. There are visionaries in this world, like Peter, and then there are the detail people, like you, I think."

I was not sure if this was a compliment or not.

"It takes both kinds of people and more to make things happen," he said, as if instructing me on how to be Peter's friend.

"So if Peter wants to make this boathouse scheme work, he needs someone like me to worry about all the details then."

"Something like that, but you have to be able to believe in the vision as well," he smiled, knowing this was not the case, at least then.

Out of nowhere came this striking figure. She rose out of the water and did a quick shiver, looking flawless standing there, staring us down.

"Hello Stuart," she said.

Stuart looked over at her. He showed no emotion, not even surprise as he responded, "Hi Danielle. Emalee, this is my cousin, Danielle." Danielle glared at me.

"Hello," I said.

"Hello," she said, then turned her gaze to Stuart, who was avoiding hers. "The boat is leaving soon, so I came to get you Stuart."

"I will be right there," he said.

"Don't take long; we have the barbeque tonight and I told my Dad I would help make some salads." I couldn't imagine this creature chopping up vegetables for a family gathering. She shrugged and abruptly left, wading, before diving in the water to swim back to their boat full of friends. She left behind a palpable tension in the air. Stuart watched her swim away and then looked over at me.

"I gotta go," he said.

"Oh, ok, no problem."

"Maybe I'll stop by your camp and you can introduce me to Peter." Everyone wanted to meet Peter.

"OK," I replied. But when? I was always frustrated by this familiar good-bye around the lake. People around the lake had a habit of saying good-bye without pinning down a date or time when they would see you again. Maybe I was anxious about this because I had said good-bye to my parents, and never saw them again. But at home, when parting from a friend, I would usually hear or say myself, 'See you on Thursday at the game;' or 'See you back at school;' or 'I'm busy the next few days, but will see you after I finish my project.' Here at the lake it was as if time did not exist. People just assumed that at some point, they would meet again and there was no good reason to set a date.

A few days later Stuart came by my camp on his boat. It was early evening and I was reading on my screened-in porch that looked out over the water. I saw him pull up in his boat and get out. He walked up to the porch and waved. How did he know I was home and not working? I didn't care. I was happy to see him again. I found it so easy and refreshing to talk with him. He did not frustrate me the way Peter did.

"Hey what's up?" He called as he walked up the shoreline. "I was boating around and thought I would see if you were in.

Audrey came out on the porch then and greeted Stuart at the door.

"Why if it isn't Stuart Lowell, all grown up," she said.

How is it she knew Stuart while I never met him until last summer?

"Last time I saw you, you were about five-years old. Your father came by to see my brother while he was visiting the lake. How is your family?"

"Fine," he replied. "My sister is getting married and my mother is all wrapped up in the planning. My dad still tinkers with boats but isn't involved with the marina at all anymore now that it's sold."

"Your family still living in Connecticut?"

"Yes, my dad likes his job there. I think he will stay

put."

"Well that is great. Can I get you a drink or something?"

"No thanks. I am fine," he replied, and looked over at me.

"Well then, I will leave you two alone," she said, smiling at me warmly for my taste in friends, and walked back into the camp.

"I thought I would meet your friend Peter," he said to me.

"OK," I said. "But first, let me take you someplace." I was not sure why, but I wanted him to see the place I watched the sun set.

I did not own a boat, as many of my summer friends did, or a car; I had a bike to get around. It was a way for me to see the surrounding environment and beautiful landscapes up-close before they were gone to development. I had one special place, discovered while riding home one day from Thendara. A dirt pathway led to the lake. Surrounded by woods, it was too tight for a car. I found a clearing in the trees, a rock ledge; I sat and watched the sunset over the lake form sunglades on the water.

We managed to get some air in the tires of my father's old bike and we biked down the road to my favorite spot. We sat on the rock ledge and looked out at the setting sun. This is usually the quietest time of the evening; you can hear the birds settling in for the night, and see the mayflies dancing over the water. It was nearing the end of their time to mate and then die; this was one of the last hatches of the summer. We did not say much, just sat considering the plight of the courting mayflies and watched the females dip their eggs into the water. Just as we were getting on our bikes to leave, a man came out of nowhere and asked us what we were doing. We were both caught off-guard.

"I bike here once in awhile to watch the sunset," I said.

"Well, this is not your property," he told us. "If you

want to watch the sunset from here, you can save $200,000 and buy your own piece of paradise." And he stalked off.

As we were heading back on our bikes Stuart said to me, "You know he's right."

"Right about what?"

"You do need to have money to own your own piece of paradise," he sighed. That thought had never occurred to me. We rode home in the gloaming.

Afterwards we headed over to Peter's camp where he and Claire were hanging out listening to music at the boathouse. Stuart's eyes lit up while Peter gave him a tour of his place, explaining all the grand plans he had for expanding. Claire and I had heard it before so we sat on the dock drinking a beer. I wanted to tell her about the place where we watched the sun set but I was too devastated to think it was now gone. There was no way I planned to go back there and face that guy again. As I was contemplating this sad fact, Stuart came up to us raving about both Peter and his work. Claire beamed.

"This place is really amazing," Stuart said.

"Yes," I said. I had heard that from so many people.

Walking back to my camp, Stuart and I got into a discussion about Peter.

"He needs to take his paintings to a gallery in some city and see if he can sell them, otherwise he will never be able to support himself through his art. These projects are a waste of his time," I said.

"There are people who just need to create," Stuart replied. "Peter is one of them. It doesn't matter to them if what they're creating has any useful value. It is probably what keeps him sane."

This struck a chord in me. Stuart must have realized, after he said it, what this statement might mean to me. I had, after all, lost my father to insanity.

"What I mean," he went on, "is that Peter would not be the same person if he was not working on some type of creative project all of the time." We reached my dock where his boat was moored. I turned to him then, reaching up to kiss him. It was hard to reach his lips because he was so tall. He leaned down, kissed and hugged me good-bye.

I lay in bed that night thinking about what Stuart said. It was true that Peter was not happy unless he was working on some project, no matter how small. He became so absorbed sometimes with his projects that it was all he could talk about. I also realized I had nothing like that to keep me occupied. While Audrey and Karl were obsessed with protecting the lake, and Claire had her writing, I was only happy when I was watching the sunset and the mayflies dance, hardly a productive endeavor. Who was I then, to judge Peter and his work?

The next day I had an AM shift at the restaurant and had to work with Dave. I had finished serving a table of six that had left me an extremely good tip when I came back to the bar to see Dave flirting with a tall, dark-haired girl. They both looked up at me when I walked over; it was Danielle, Dave was flirting with Danielle! I caught them in the middle of some inside joke, and when they saw me they quieted down. I glanced over at Danielle to acknowledge her and she gave me a quick nod but no greeting.

As I was adding up the bill in my head, Dave yelled at me, "Why don't you get a freakin' calculator?" He looked at Danielle and laughed.

I blushed, tried to think of something to say in reply "I like to use my head," I said.

Great comeback I thought. I wished Claire were there, she would know just what to say to Dave. Just then, she breezed in.

"What's this about a calculator?" she said so everyone at the bar could hear.

"Oh, nothing," Dave responded, glancing at me. "About time you got here, I have to go. The bar is stocked," he said. After several graduation brunches and no stocked bar, Dave had admitted defeat. Danielle, clearly bored now that Dave's attention was not on her, got up to leave. Dave gave her a look that said, I'll be right with you.

"Robbing the cradle aren't we Dave?" Claire remarked after Danielle left.

"Fuck you Claire," he retorted.

"You wish," she smiled at him sarcastically.

Dave left in a huff. Claire rooted through her bag while I was adding up my bill and threw a small calculator over to me.

"Here, keep it," she said, "but don't let Dave know. He hates to think you and I are smarter than him."

Claire had a secret disdain for people like Dave that didn't have a college degree — which was rather ironic considering that Peter, her new love interest, never completed his. Dave was one of the local boys from the town of Canandaigua. Guys like Dave never wanted to leave the lake. They would spend their summers here working at the resorts or vineyards, and when things closed down for the season, head south to make money in the winter months so they could buy fishing tackle, bait, and keep their motor-boat running for the summer on the lake. He tried to take a few classes at the community college, realized that there were no jobs that would allow him so much flexibility, and quit school.

Claire looked disheveled, which was not like her. She pulled a make-up kit and hairbrush out of her bag, shook her long black hair out of its bun and asked me to fill in at the bar while she ran to the bathroom to get herself in order.

"What's with you?" I asked when she came back.

"Spent the night at Peter's and just lay around all day; lost track of the time."

That was easy to do with Peter, just sit around all day dreaming up ideas, especially for someone like Claire who needed them for her writing.

"How is your writing going?" I asked.

She laughed. "Not much happening on that end since I met Peter." Clearly, they did enjoy each other's company. I could not recall, in all the years that I had known Peter, him ever having a serious relationship with anyone but me. And we weren't intimate. I never stayed the night at his house unless we came home late from a party on the lake and I didn't want to disturb Audrey. Even then, I slept in his loft while he slept on the floor. I wasn't sure if I was jealous that Peter had found a lover, or relieved.

"A piece of advice to you Emalee," Claire interrupted my thoughts, "stay away from that girl."

"Who? Danielle? I hardly know her. She is Stuart's cousin."

"I know who she is, and I know she is Stuart's 'kissing cousin.' I'm telling you there is something off about that girl."

"How would you know that Claire?"

"Emalee, I just know things. I'm a bartender, I hear everything that happens around this lake, whether I want to or not. Give people a few drinks and before you know it they're telling you more than you want to know, or you overhear it anyway. Believe me, that girl is a soul crusher."

I couldn't tell if it was Claire's warning that had me paranoid, or if what she said about Danielle was true, but for the next two weeks, it seemed Danielle was always showing up at the restaurant during my shifts. Although she hardly acknowledged my presence, I felt she was stalking me. The first few times she came by, Dave was working, and she immediately focused her attention on him. She was obviously over twenty-one, because he plied her with alcohol as she sat languidly on the bar stool, leaning over to whisper in his ear while he poured her drinks. If Dave wasn't around, she would order a drink anyway and take it out onto the deck. She would sit by herself looking out at the lake.

This went on for a while until the day Stuart showed up to see me. He must have called the camp, or stopped by to see if I was around, and Audrey told him I was at the restaurant working. I was just starting my PM shift with Claire when he came in and went right up to me to ask how I was doing.

"Fine," I said. "What're you doing here?"

"I came to see if you wanted to get together this week sometime. Do you have a day off?"

Just then Danielle walked in.

"Dave isn't here, " I called to her. Dave had taken the day off. She probably knew that. It was clear to me she was not here to see Dave.

"Hello Stuart; fancy meeting you here," she said to Stuart, before turning to me, "Dave isn't around today? What a shame, I was hoping to talk to him." Because she was tall, she had this habit of looking right over me while she feigned addressing me directly; it made me feel small. Stuart was tall too, but he looked me in the eye.

"You know by now that Dave has every Tuesday off, given all the time you're spending with him," chimed in Claire. "What do you really want?" Good old Claire cutting to the chase.

Danielle glared at her, "I want to have a drink with my cousin. Stuart, would you have a drink with me?"

Sensing the tension, Stuart agreed to a drink with her. "I'll bring out a couple of beers; meet me on the deck Danielle," he instructed her.

She demurely complied. Stuart turned to me when she left, "What day do you have off? I can adjust my schedule at the marina."

"How about Thursday?" I said.

"Great, see you then." He took two beers from Claire, paid his bill and went to meet Danielle on the deck. I stayed away from them but could tell they were having a heated discussion. After one beer, they left.

Stuart picked me up at the crack of dawn that Thursday morning. He had a canoe on his father's truck. We headed south towards the beautiful rolling hills in the town of Naples. Once in town, Stuart took a turn into the entrance for the State High Tor Wildlife Preserve. We took the canoe off the truck and launched it in the West River, a meandering scenic waterway that leads to the lake. It was a still morning, the sun was rising in the sky and it was going to be a hot day. The water had a green sheen, a blanket of duckweed floating on top of it. Our canoe easily slid over the small aquatic plant. As we wound our way through the waters of the West River we saw a muskrat scrambling down the bank, a Great Blue heron calmly stalking the water's edge looking for breakfast, and numerous fish. We kept gliding along until we reached a marsh. The sedges and rushes were so tall they scraped the canoe while we floated amongst them. As we sat in the forest of rushes our senses were treated to all kinds of natural sights and sounds; we saw a red-winged blackbird flitting from stem to stem, creaking out his 'oakleeeeee' call to announce his territory, the 'garumph' of the bullfrogs, the 'plop' of turtles jumping from logs into the water when our canoe disturbed their sunning. Fish were jumping, and dragonflies were hovering over the lily pads looking for an insect to eat.

Slowly we worked our way up the lazy river to the southern end of the lake.

Where the river ends the wide expanse of the lake is framed by the steep hills, formed by glaciers thousands of years ago, a view best seen from the water.

"You don't have to have $200,000 to view this," I said.

"Nope," Stuart replied. "As a matter of fact, the state is trying to preserve more of this land around the southern end." He waved his hands in the air to take in the land they were trying to save. "They're trying to buy it from landowners and keep it in the preserve, I think they're working with the Finger Lakes Land Trust."

I had heard about the Finger Lakes Land Trust before, Audrey and Karl had mentioned them in one of their conversations about protecting the land from development at the southern end. These acres were wanted for their views. I always found it ironic when Karl brought up preserving the land in the southern end because his camp was on one of these steep cliffs, built long ago, but still, on the same cliffs he was trying to keep others off.

The trust purchases land outright or development rights from willing property owners. Depending on the deal they make, it can be left undeveloped, or the owners continue to use the land as they like (such as farming), but with the agreement that it will not be developed. The landowners then have the ability to write off the donation on their taxes, or in the case that they still live on the land and use it for their own purposes, their taxes are lower because it's not valued as much for development.

Back at the truck we put the canoe in, and headed to Stuart's camp. Situated on a small knoll, his camp was more like a house. It had long since been upgraded so that they could use it year-round if they wanted, although no one did. A short set of stairs led up to the main floor. The entrance came right into the kitchen, with a great room beyond it. The great room had floor-to-ceiling windows covering the whole width of the room and looked out over the lake. Attached to the great room was a deck. Upstairs were small bedrooms, and downstairs, the master bedroom with windows the width of the house. They had a great view of the eastern side of the lake and I could imagine seeing the sunrise from there.

He went to grab some beers from the refrigerator, and I went to sit on his deck looking over the lake. While I was waiting for my drink I noticed a pink paperback book on a table, *Zen and the Art of Motorcycle Maintenance: An Inquiry into Values, 25th edition.* I picked it up and came across this passage first:

We're in such a hurry most of the time we never get much chance to talk. The result is a kind of endless day-to-day shallowness, a monotony that leaves a person wondering years later where all the time went and sorry that it's all gone.

Stuart came out to the deck and saw me reading his book. "That was one of my required readings for a philosophy course," he said as he handed me my beer.

"What's it about?" I asked.

"It's about a man, he's a professor of philosophy actually, and he has a breakdown when he spends too much time thinking about things, specifically, what is the meaning of quality. After his treatment, to make up for lost time, he takes his son on a motorcycle trip across country," Stuart explained. "Of course," he added, while looking at me with a small smile, "that's an over-simplification. It's a bit more complicated than that. That's why I'm reading it again."

"Sounds deep," I said, and put the book down. "Is that what philosophers do, just sit around and think about things? Wouldn't that be boring? I can see why someone might go insane."

Although I hated talking about insanity, and what the mind can do to people, I felt compelled to ask Stuart why he studied philosophy. It seemed like a big waste of time to me, kind of like one of Peter's endless projects.

"Well, you like to look at nature right?" Stuart asked me. "You know, the earliest philosophers were considered natural philosophers because they were trying to figure out how the world worked. It was not until Newton came along and put math formulas to his theories that people started to believe empirical science was *the* way to understand how the world works. Philosophy is the art of thinking about thinking. You deconstruct thought and language to get to the larger truths."

"Hmmm," I responded. What I didn't tell him was,

that when I got inside my head too much, I became undone because of my grief. So instead, I contemplated the natural beauty of the world around me, the objectivity in that kept me sane. "I only know about the scientific method: you observe, come up with a hypothesis, experiment, and draw conclusions based on the data. It's a rational and objective way to view the world."

"So it works for you Emalee, but not everybody wants to look at the world that way. Peter for instance, he definitely looks at the world differently — he observes things not for what they are but for what they could become. It's like everything for him is a blank canvas."

"So what *do* philosophers talk about? I mean you and I can talk about friends like Peter and Claire, or the weather, or the lake, and that makes sense. But why spend time talking about things you can't ever fully understand such as power, greed, or death?"

"Well, let's take love for example."

I was intrigued. I hadn't expected him to follow-up with such an intimate subject.

"It's a feeling we all know, but do we really know it? In a book called Phaedrus, written by Plato over 2,000 years ago…"

"Wait," I interrupted, "you mean to tell me you're reading books that are over 2,000 years old?"

Stuart looked my way, "Yes, I am." He laughed. "Anyway, in the book Socrates is having a dialogue with Phaedrus. Socrates talks about the human dilemma with love, that is, do you submit to your base desires when you find something beautiful? Or do you manage your longings so as to enable that beauty to flourish?"

"What does that mean exactly, allowing beauty to flourish? Isn't something either beautiful or not beautiful? And isn't it really up to the person viewing the object to decide whether it's beautiful or not?"

"Well, I don't know, but think of beauty as a state of mind then, a yearning, and the potential in all of us to misuse or control our base desires."

"I don't get it." I kicked my feet up onto the small table and took a swig of my beer.

"Ok, then think of it this way: there are two types of love; there is the exploitative kind of love, the kind where one person, or both are motivated by lust or power; control, really. This type of love doesn't usually lead anywhere. It doesn't benefit anyone, just satisfies the basest of desires. Not beautiful, you might say."

I blushed, thinking about the young man from the Chateau. Did Stuart know about my tryst? How could he?

"Then," he continued, "there is the kind of love that is non-exploitative. This love is about guidance, caring, and mentoring. It's a love two people share when the intent isn't so much selfish, as selfless. It requires a person to think; not about himself, but how his love can manifest itself by making the other a better person for having known him. Beautiful." He looked out over the water as he emphasized this point, his hands pointing towards the lake as if it knew what he was talking about. "We struggle all the time with this dilemma, that is, what to do about love."

Then he turned towards me and his eyes bored into mine. I was not sure what he was aiming at but the conversation was making me uneasy. So I decided to change the subject.

"Your cousin Danielle has been hanging out at the restaurant a lot lately. Are you two close?" I think it was a dig. He was so sure of himself, and I wanted him to question his own feelings as I was questioning mine.

Stuart's mood changed. He looked out at the lake and clenched his teeth. "She and I grew up together, we have spent every summer together here." He looked at me. "I don't know why she is hanging out at the restaurant where you work, and I don't care, but I doubt she wants to be your friend or anything like that."

We both sat quietly and looked out over the lake.

"I better get you home, I have to check on a boat at the marina," he said.

I thought he had the day off.

He led me out of the house and took me home. I guessed bringing Danielle into the conversation put an end to it. Claire was right. Soul crusher indeed.

Audrey and Karl were talking at the kitchen table and looked up when we came in. Karl gave Stuart a handshake.

"How are your folks doing?" he asked Stuart.

"Oh, fine, they're coming up this weekend. All of my aunts and uncles are coming, to talk about the land."

"We were just discussing that ourselves," Karl motioned to us to sit at the table.

"They're under a lot of pressure to sell," Stuart said, sitting down, "and they're being offered a lot of money."

"What for?" Audrey laughed. "The developers can't use it anyway, the town will never allow them to build their own sewer facility."

"You'd be surprised, Audrey," Karl said. "There are a few members of the Town council that are willing to hear proposals. There are new technologies called cluster septic systems that are feasible for this site if they can get the land and the Town wants the tax revenue just like the developer wants the money."

"I wish they would keep the land; it's the last parcel of the Lowell property, but I don't have much say in any of it." Stuart sounded resigned to the fact that the land was as good as sold.

Karl did not want to put him on the spot anymore than they had. He got up and put his arm around Stuart's shoulder. "You know Stuart, I've been meaning to talk to you about an old Penn Yan my friend owns that needs a total re-hab," he said, as he walked him to the door.

Stuart looked back at me and smiled, "See you later," he said, walking out to the truck with Karl.

I went up to my room and called Laurel. The day had ended too abruptly for me and I needed to do something. It was a hot, gorgeous summer day and Laurel would know how to cheer me up. She was not an intellectual like Stuart, not eccentric like Claire and Peter. She was easy to be with, and lots of fun. We could laugh at anything together. We went to the cove in her boat to hang out with friends and swim. We were having a streak of hot weather and warm nights and the lake was getting warmer.

It was refreshing to swim; the lake had a clean smell to it that day. Laurel and I used to talk about bottling that smell and calling it *Lake*, a perfume or air freshener we would market and sell to the local tourists to take home with them to remember the lake. We would laugh about it sometimes when we tried to figure out how to describe that particular smell, a sense you get when you first come to the surface of the water from the depths below. Was it fish? Rotting seaweed? Cool air that lies right at the surface? We never could describe it accurately; we just knew it was there. After swimming at the cove all day, we all decided to meet at the Owly-Out that evening.

Laurel picked me up later in her car, and we drove to the Owly-Out. It was a steamy night, and the place was packed. All of the townies and summer folk were making a night of it before the crush of weekend tourists. The jukebox was blasting and we immediately grabbed a beer and started to dance with our friends. This went on for a while before I started to feel dizzy and went to the bar to get some water. While I was sitting there I saw Danielle stumble into the bar. She was alone, as usual, and I wondered, did this girl have any friends? She was drunk. I smugly noted she did not have her usual cool composure. She eyed the place, overlooking me of course, and spotted Dave sitting with his friends and a bunch of girls at a booth in the corner. She wove across the bar to where he was talking and slapped him hard across the face. Even with the jukebox playing, people watched the scene unfold.

"What the fuck?" Dave yelled at her and grabbed her wrists before she could strike again.

"You fucking bastard," she screamed. He hauled her out of the bar and they proceeded to yell at each other in the parking lot outside. He came back into the bar without her, looking around to see if anyone noticed his embarrassment just when I happened to be looking at him. He glared at me, and stalked back over to his friends in the booth. They quickly gave him his beer and consoled him. I heard him call her a fucking bitch, and I felt sorry for Danielle at that moment.

She came back in, and ignoring Dave, wobbled over to sit down in a booth on the other side of the bar. She reached into her bag and grabbed a bright red Nokia cell phone and called someone.

Laurel came up to me at the bar and grabbed my arm. "Come on, quit gawking at them. They're a buzz kill, all of them."

We went back to the dance floor, but my heart wasn't in it. I kept my eye on Danielle to make sure she did not have car keys in her hand and planned to drive herself anywhere. I didn't have to worry though because soon after, Stuart walked in. He went over to Danielle, barely able to hold her head up by then, and gently holding her elbow, maneuvered her out of the bar. He never saw me.

That night I thought a lot about Stuart. What was he to me exactly? He did not fit into any of the categories I had so far for guys. I did not want to have a fling with him and forget about him. I knew that if we were to have sex and that happened, I would be very sad. But I did not think of him as just a friend either. No, he meant more to me than that. Was I falling for him? I was also perplexed by his relationship with his cousin. She obviously depended on Stuart for something; his friendship, his love perhaps? Did they share some kind of intimate secret? Why was she always showing up whenever I was around? Was it by chance, because I worked with Dave? Or was it because I was getting too close to Stuart? She was an anomaly I did not want to figure out.

CHAPTER FIVE

Mayfly nymphs go through only partial change of form as they increase in size. They shed their inelastic outside skeleton at intervals through their nymphal lives. After each molt the nymph grows for a period, then sheds its skin again, and in mayflies this may go on for twenty times or more. — Ann Haven Morgan

It was mid-July and the days of the mayfly hatches were coming to an end. I hadn't seen a swarm at dusk in quite a while. The eggs were laid and had fallen to the bottom of the lake to start a new cycle of life under water until next year when the winged adults would emerge and begin the courtship flight again.

There was still a bit of summer left to enjoy before I had to head back to school and I wanted to spend as much of it as I could with Stuart. I asked him if he wanted to come with me, Claire, Peter, and Laurel to a concert at the Finger Lakes Performing Arts Center. We were planning to see the Dave Matthews Band perform. He agreed and on a beautiful starlit night we arrived on the lawn of the Center and spread out some blankets. We drank wine and danced to the music. It was a great time until Laurel started to feel sick. She had had too much to drink that night, and wine was not her preferred beverage. She looked green as I walked her to the bathrooms. We were standing in line when Danielle appeared out of nowhere.

"Looks like someone is not feeling all that well," she remarked looking down at Laurel who was flopping at my side. "Is Stuart with you?" she asked me.

I did not want Danielle to ruin my night even if Laurel was cutting into my fun, but it was hard to lie to her, she scared me. "Yes," I replied. I didn't tell her where we were sitting.

"Figures," she said with a taint of disgust.

"Why do you care?" I asked her. She leveled her gaze on me.

"He's my cousin. I just want to know who he's hanging with, that's all. You two do spend a lot of time together don't you? How do you even know him?"

Just then Laurel groaned, "I really don't feel well," she said. She leaned over and to my despair, threw-up all over Danielle's perfectly manicured toes and expensive leather sandals.

I dragged Laurel back to the blanket where we were all sitting, and made her lie down. She immediately fell to sleep. 'Good,' I thought, it gave me a chance to enjoy the rest of the concert. Stuart held me and we swayed to the music. The whole night was starlit and magical, as if it were made for us to enjoy, and no one, not even Danielle, could interfere.

After the concert we dropped Laurel off at her camp and went back to mine. Audrey and Karl joined us on the porch. We all sat looking out at the lake, the chairs lined up in a horse-shoe. Every once in a while I would look over and catch Stuart smiling at me, such a happy smile, such a comforting thing.

Audrey and Karl stayed up as late as they could, then said good night. Karl was staying over. We all just kept talking, Peter about his latest paintings; he had been contacted by one of the professors he knew from his university days. He hadn't lasted long as a student; he didn't need others to teach him his craft (so he said). This professor must have seen something in his work because he had a connection with a gallery in Cleveland that was willing to show some of his paintings. We all encouraged him to pursue it but he was somewhat vague on the details.

Claire talked about how she was not writing enough, but had recently discovered poetry as an outlet for her talents. "I find myself spinning off these random thoughts that turn into poems. They may not be that good but I am going with it for now," she said. Her plans to attend graduate school at NYU in the fall were coming together.

Stuart told us funny stories about his roommates in college that were, as he said, brilliant, although they barely made it to classes for all of the partying they did. His friends sounded elitist to me, but what did I know? He talked about his plans to go on for a PhD in Philosophy and was sending out inquiries to universities all over the world. Being a couple of years behind them all, I did not have any grand plans for the following fall other than attending school.

"I just plan to finish my degree on time," I said. "So many of my classmates are studying for their medical school exams. I don't think that is what I want to do with my biology degree."

"You should study nature," Claire said dryly. "You spend so much time in it."

Claire and I had shared some laughs about the patrons at the restaurant, but we steered clear of any conversation about Dave or Danielle. At one point Peter looked over at my feet that were resting on the coffee table.

"Is that the normal color of your feet?" he asked.

I looked down at them. They were a bluish purple; the blood had stopped circulating from the long night of sitting. Then, suddenly, the barn swallows came to life.

They circled by the porch, doing their acrobatics in the air, catching insects after a long night of not eating, in and out of the boathouse they flew, giving us a show. The sun was rising. We had stayed up all night and hadn't even realized it. I glanced over at Stuart, our eyes locked on each other and for a brief moment, I sensed it, a longing for something, but what? Where was this relationship going and how would it end once the summer was over? I looked away from him. It was the beginning of a brand new day; I didn't want to think about endings.

What I couldn't stop thinking about, however, was Stuart. He was always on my mind. I kept waiting for the next chance to see him. I was so taken by the idea of seeing him that I uncharacteristically asked to go with Audrey to one of the lake association meetings, hoping he'd be there. The meeting that night was on the his family's proposed land sale across the road from the marina project.

The meeting was being held at the town Grange Hall. It was packed — people were standing in the back of the room when we walked in. Karl was there and had saved a seat for us. He motioned for us to come forward and sit. We had a pretty good view of the front. There, at a table facing the audience, was Stuart's father, Bob (I could see a resemblance), his Uncle Mark, and a member of the lake association. Next to them was a big map of the development plans for the marina and a diagram showing the plans for the Lowells' property across the road. I came hoping to see Stuart, and ended up getting an education on sewage treatment.

The lake association representative spoke first, asking everyone to quiet down so he could speak to the crowd. "First I want to thank Bob and Mark Lowell for agreeing to come tonight to speak to us. I also want to remind everyone that nothing has been finalized yet and we need to listen with open minds to the Lowells. They did not have to come here tonight at all so I expect everyone to show them the courtesy of listening to them before speaking out," he said.

Bob and Mark Lowell looked at the crowd with no expression in their eyes. I saw the same self-assuredness in Stuart's father as I often saw in Stuart. He spoke first. "I want everyone to understand," he said softly, "that we have as much interest in protecting this lake as you all do. We also have to consider our family's interest, and when I say family, I'm not just speaking about Mark and myself. This issue also involves our other two brothers, and collectively the fourteen nieces and nephews that all have a stake in this land. As you know, the developers of the marina approached us asking to purchase twenty acres across the road so they can move forward with their plans. Without this land deal they will not be able to develop the property the way they want, that is, to have as many houses or a clubhouse for the owners. The land doesn't drain well and they don't have enough of it to build as many houses as they would like."

There was a lot of mumbling in the crowd at this point. The man from the lake association waved his hand for quiet.

I scanned the room looking for Stuart. Was he here? I thought he would take an interest in this, but I didn't see him anywhere. In fact, from my observations of the audience, I was the only person in the place under the age of fifty. I saw Dr. and Mrs. Smith, he, retired from a practice in Canandaigua; the Youngs, both of them lawyers from Rochester; and Mrs. Langtry, owner of a print shop in Rochester. There were many other folks that I recognized, patrons of the restaurant; they lived in the city of Canandaigua or in the towns nearby.

"Mark and I met with the developers, and as you can see from this map and diagram they gave us, they want to build twenty houses on the lakeside, turn the marina into a clubhouse for private use, and allow lake access to all of the owners. In order to do this, they need the land for a leach field. They do not have enough land favorable for leach fields, and they're too far to annex to the city of Canandaigua's sewer system. Their plans are to install what is called a 'cluster system'. This is a newer technology, used in rural areas where there is a need for septic systems to dispose of the home waste but not enough land. With the cluster system, the houses collect the waste in a tank underground, and then the 'gray water', or leftover waste water, is pumped to an open field where it can leach into the soil." He pointed to the diagram showing the underground tanks outside each new house and the clubhouse, tanks, and a string of pipes leading from each to leach fields across the road on the Lowells' property.

Although I knew when I flushed the toilet, ran the dishwasher, or did the laundry at the camp that my waste went somewhere to a place called a 'septic system', I never knew exactly what that was. Some of the older camps like mine had signs everywhere, 'don't flush this or that down the toilet', 'do not use this type of detergent', 'not good for the septic'. It amazed me how primitive the systems were. Once the laundry was done, the wastewater ran into a tank underground, where the solid stuff sinks, and the rest of it, or 'gray water' as Stuart's father was calling it, went into pipes that filtered it into the soil — the leach field.

"What happens to the land then? Does it just become used for a sewer system?" someone shouted out. There were calls in agreement.

"Now wait a minute," Stuart's Uncle Mark, interjected, to calm the crowd. "This land has the potential to be developed into a bunch of housing or it can be left as open space. Even if there are leach lines running through it, this cluster septic is no different than what all of you have right now in front of your own camps. Even better, this system will be new, and that is more than I can say about some of the systems that are right up to the water's edge around here."

People went quiet then. They all knew that he was right about that; many dreaded the day when the health inspector came knocking on their door wanting to check if the septic was working. Most of the systems around the lake had been grandfathered in, as they were passed down in the family. Some systems were over fifty years old, and there was more than one camp owner that would go to the laundromat a week before the inspectors came, instead of washing at home, just to keep the system dry. A failed septic system could cost a cottage owner a lot of money, and it was state law that they fix it. After all, the lake provides drinking water for the city and surrounding towns. The state can't allow raw sewage to pollute the supply.

"As you all know," Bob Lowell said, "land values around here are skyrocketing, and so are the taxes. We lease to farmers now but they don't want to buy it. They can find good land cheaper, farther from the lake, and without as many restrictions on what they do. If we don't sell the land to these guys, we may have to sell to someone else who will just come along and build houses on it. The views up there are worth a lot of money right now. Heck, even some of our children are saying they want to build there. So what it boils down to is: what is good for this land, as well as for our family? Because one way or another, this developer is going to figure out how to get his houses built with a private clubhouse at the marina. He needs to do something, because the marina is not paying the mortgage he has on the land right now, and the taxes have got to be bankrupting him."

I looked over at Karl who was stewing in his seat, one of the only times I ever saw him not speak up about the issue. I attributed his composure to his friendship with the Lowells. I had overheard him talk to Audrey about his relationship with Mark and another, older brother. He knew this family very well; they had spent many summers on the lake, swimming in the same coves I did, they may even have been the ones responsible for the rope swing on the water for all I knew. I imagine he was trying not to offend them, and was keeping his comments to himself until he had a chance to talk to them privately.

Another association member got up to ask some questions. "And what about the marina development? I know your family sold it years ago, but if we allow this development to happen, then there goes one of the few remaining public access sites on the lake. As it is, you can hardly get a spot at the state launch to put your boat in the water and the Lowells' Marina was always a place people could put their boat in the water for a few bucks." People murmured in agreement, the loss of the marina to a private club and housing was a bigger loss to some of them than the view of the lake. It was like the amusement park all over again, another lake icon lost to history.

We left the meeting in a somber mood, me because I was dwelling on where Stuart might be, and Audrey and Karl because of the outcome. I don't think either of them liked what the Lowell brothers had to say about the land sale. It all seemed inevitable to me. What other choice did they have? At least the developer planned to keep the twenty acres across the road as open space, and according to what I heard at the meeting that night, they even offered to have public access trails, and spots for visitors to park their cars and hike into the fields to enjoy the view. I was curious to see this land everyone was so worked up about.

And that was my excuse to see Stuart again. I got on my bike a few days later and biked over to the marina, hoping to find him and ask him for a tour of the Lowell land. I biked the ten miles or so around the north end of the lake to the other side, and watched him talking with a customer who had just driven up in his boat. They were discussing some issue with the engine. I got off my bike and leaned it against the side of the marina building, sat on a bench and waited for them to be finished. Stuart waved at me and went back to talking with the customer. The guy he was talking with looked vaguely familiar to me, then he turned around to leave, and I saw him. It was the young man from the Chateau. I had no other choice but to acknowledge him. He came right up to me.

"Well if it isn't the girl and her bike," he said. What a jerk, I thought. He took hold of one of my hands. "How are you?" He asked me, looking right into my eyes as if we had some intimate secret.

"Just fine," I replied, looking away. I wanted to remove my hand from his but was trying to remain casual.

"I haven't seen you all summer; where've you been?" Really? He had to know he could find me if he wanted to, he had, after all, picked me up at my camp once. He didn't wait for me to answer. "Well, I've got to go," he said, looking up at his ride. "I can't wait to see you again," he squeezed my hand, "I will look you up." He waved at me as he jumped into the waiting car; I noticed there was a girl about my age driving.

I stood there, embarrassed. Stuart, saw the whole encounter. "You know that guy?" he asked me.

"Sort of." I watched the car roll on to the highway. Stuart looked at me levelly, and then smiled as he looked away. He could tell I was lying.

"Well, I hope not too well," he said condescendingly while he looked down at the boat. He climbed in to take out the keys and a few other items. "He's not the sharpest tool in the shed. Wouldn't know the difference between a fuel pump and a carburetor."

I quickly changed the subject. "I came to see your property." That encounter had me unnerved, I was so sure before I came of my intention to spend time with Stuart and tell him how I felt, but I was not so sure if he would respond in kind, and I did not want to take that risk. Now that whole idea seemed stupid to me, as I stood there, with no idea whether Stuart could take time away from his job to give me a tour of the land across the road, and it was my only lure to get him to talk to me.

Stuart looked up at me with a curious glance. "Ok," he said. He did not ask any more questions. He put his tools away and walked over to me. "Follow me," he said.

The marina sits on the lake, and above the marina were fields, some woods, and the parking lot. Boaters wanting to use the marina had plenty of options to park their cars and trailers. They access the marina from West Lake Road, drop their boats in the water and for a fee, park their trailers and cars in the lot for the day. Some people paid a seasonal fee to keep their boats in slips all summer, and the marina would seal the boats and store them in the lot for the winter for an additional fee. Many of the people in town used the marina, especially those that didn't have any other lake access. When Stuart's family sold the marina and the land that came with it, they probably never thought it would be anything but a marina. The land around it had once been farmed, but it was sloped and there were drainage issues as well. A farmer was leasing parts of it now to grow hay. The rest was a woodlot, harvested at least once for valuable tree species such as oak, maple and ash.

We walked up the dirt road leading out of the marina and onto West Lake Road, looked both ways, and crossed to Stuart's land, the last parcel in the Lowell legacy. A small path mowed in the fields of Timothy-grass took us along a shallow creek. As we traveled up the path, the land became steeper and the grass gave way to woodlands. The creek was now in a ravine, and we looked down the steep sides to see the water tumbling over large rocks, creating small waterfalls and pools.

"I used to spend a lot of time down there, catching crayfish with my brother and sister, and cousins. Your favorite insect lives down there too." He looked at me. "The mayflies live under the rocks in the creek all year until they hatch in the summer."

"Really?" I said, "and how do you know that?"

"Because we used to find them crawling under rocks. My dad told me what they were. They spend their youth as aquatic creatures, kind of like frogs spend their time as tadpoles before becoming frogs. Mayflies have gills while they live under water." I wondered how he, a philosopher, knew so much about nature.

He led me up to a point where there was a large rock — an *erratic*, a glacial remnant, cast off when the glaciers were receding into the north — perched along the side of the hill. We leaned against it and looked out over the view. It was spectacular. I could understand why someone would want to build a house, right here, to see the sunrise over the lake every morning. I said this to Stuart.

He sighed, "I know, I always thought that's what I would do in this exact spot, build a home and watch the sunrise. But I'm not sure what is going to happen now."

I could only imagine the turmoil that this land sale was causing within the family. With fourteen cousins, dividing this land up between them for housing would ruin the view, and the beauty of the place. It needed to stay as it was, in my opinion, there were so few places like this left around the lake and it wasn't fair for someone to keep it all to themselves.

Stuart had to get back to work. He seemed reluctant to say good-bye to me. I knew I did not want to say good-bye to him. But he left me in typical fashion, without any commitment as to when he and I would see each other again. I rode back to my camp in a foul mood. Why couldn't I just admit to him how I felt anyway? What was holding me back? What was holding him back? I knew he had feelings for me, he just wouldn't admit it. As I passed Peter's camp I decided to stop in and see him, thinking maybe he could brighten my mood. At least he would provide a diversion from my constant thinking about Stuart.

I found him, for the first time in quite a while, without Claire. He was working on the roof of his boathouse. He climbed down when he saw me and brought me inside. He wanted to show me his latest painting. It was a self-portrait of him and Claire, the faces were a bit distorted, on purpose, and the background was the lake. I remember that the palette of colors he chose for the background were very bright, almost drawing attention away from the faces. I was both intrigued and startled by the painting, not sure which emotion was winning out.

Seeing this painting made me think of all of the others he had sitting around in his parents' attic.

"Whatever happened to the gallery showing in Cleveland?" I asked him.

"Oh, I told my professor friend that I wanted to wait and see."

"Wait for what?" I asked, my frustration with him rising.

"I think my stuff is too good for a small gallery in Cleveland. I need to go to New York City."

"And who is opening doors for you in New York, Peter? Why aren't you jumping at this chance to show your work to somebody in Cleveland while you have it?"

Peter avoided my stare. He was looking at his artwork, at anything but me, who didn't believe in him.

"I think I can manage it Emalee, even if you don't think so."

"Oh yeah, and what is it you are afraid of? People actually seeing your work? I mean Peter, you spend hours working on these projects for whom? Yourself? Maybe it's time for you to put yourself out there, stop talking about your dreams and make them happen."

He glanced over at me. For the first time ever, I think he was angry with me.

"You know Emalee, you are really good at telling me what I should and shouldn't do, but you don't exactly 'put yourself out there' either. I mean when was the last time you talked about your true feelings about something? You can't even talk about your parents. In the past five years since their death I have never heard you talk about them, or what happened, and how it's affected you. It's like you have no feelings at all."

We glared at each other, I think he had wanted to tell me this for a long time, and it took his anger to get it all out. He was not sorry for it either; he knew he had hurt me and he left me standing there in his house, while he walked out and continued working on his roof. I left in tears, not saying good-bye. I knew he was right.

CHAPTER SIX

Mayflies spend nearly all of their lives as nymphs in the water. — Ann Haven Morgan

A few days later I was working with Claire at the restaurant. I wasn't sure if Peter had told her about our argument and I didn't want to talk about it. But at some point during the hectic day she stopped me and said, "Emalee, I hope you are ok with Peter coming to New York with me."

"New York?" Peter hadn't told me he was going to New York with *her*, just that he wanted to go to New York.

"Yes, well, my parents are putting me up in a flat in the City while I get my master's degree and I asked Peter to come along. My family has connections in the art world in New York and I thought I might be able to introduce Peter to some gallery owners."

So that was what Peter failed to mention. Why wouldn't he have told me it was Claire opening doors for him in New York?

"I think that's great," I said to her. And I meant it sincerely, because Peter deserved a chance. He needed

Claire to help him and that was more than I had ever been able to do for him. Claire believed in Peter more than I did, and deep down I had a nagging feeling that I had let Peter down.

That day proved to be full of surprises. Karl came into the restaurant to have lunch with a woman who looked to be in her early thirties. They were talking intimately while dining. I was curious to know why Karl didn't seek me out. When I got back to the camp, Karl was down by the water talking with the woman and Audrey. I approached them at the lakefront. They looked up at me from their chairs.

"Why hello," Karl said. "There is someone I want you to meet."

The woman stood up to greet me. "Hi, I'm Karl's daughter, Mary," she said as she took my hand.

I was in shock, disbelief, that this important fact about Karl, that he had a family, was never revealed to me before. "Nice to meet you," I said, regaining my composure. "Excuse me for staring, I guess I am just shocked to hear that Karl has a daughter, I never knew."

"Well," she said, looking around at Karl and Audrey, "It was never convenient, I guess." She smiled at me weakly, "I have to go. I hope we meet again." And without further explanation of why she chose now to enter my life, she left.

There was an awkward silence between Audrey and me as Karl walked his daughter to her car. I looked to her for some type of explanation.

"Karl can explain it," was all Audrey said, and she climbed into her sunfish to take a sail. Karl came back and motioned for me to sit down next to him. We looked out on the lake as he told me his story. He had always been in love with Audrey, ever since they were young. But when he went off to college, his father sold the camp, and Karl rarely came back to the lake after that. Audrey had moved on; she found a new love at college and got married. Three years later he died, but by then Karl himself was married.

He settled down in Philadelphia, got into real estate development there, and had a family. But he always thought about Audrey and the lake. He knew one day he would come back. When the sale of a small camp at the southern end came around for a good price, he bought it. That was twenty years ago. He renovated the camp and brought his family up but his wife never took to the place. She was from the city and did not like swimming in the lake, did not like the bugs at the camp. He continued to come to the lake though, usually on his own, sometimes with his daughter. His wife didn't seem to care, and let him cnjoy his solitudc.

About ten years before I arrived on the scene, he ran into Audrey at the store; he had not seen her in years. They immediately became good friends again. One thing led to another, and he found himself wanting to come back to the lake more often, just to see Audrey. It was around the time I showed up in Audrey's life that his wife became ill with cancer. He spent many days with her at the hospital, and to get away from the pain and grief of it all, he would escape to the lake and Audrey while his daughter took care of her mother.

"It was a time in my life when I didn't know what to do. I was so grief stricken that my wife was going to die, and so in love with your aunt. I felt such guilt about everything I was doing. Audrey helped me get through it all," he said. "My wife died about two years ago."

"Why didn't you tell me about all of this before?" I asked him.

"Well, we thought about it, but you will learn, Emalee, as I have, that sometimes you have to keep things to yourself until you know that the timing is right."

How true, I thought. I am not sure I would have been able to handle Karl's double life when I first came to live with Audrey, not after all that I had been through with my parents' death. I just couldn't believe that Karl was able to keep his own grief locked away inside and never reveal that he had a family sequestered away in Philadelphia. He showed me pictures of his family, his grandchild, Mary's son. And now I understood why Audrey and he were always so evasive about their relationship. I felt a huge relief inside to know the truth, and felt so happy that they were able to love each other after all those years and all the obstacles placed between them.

I left Karl on the beach to wait for Audrey, thinking that I would talk to her later, while Karl wasn't around. I also wanted to see Peter, and apologize. I walked over to his place and found him and Stuart sitting together on his dock drinking a beer. Stuart looked at me and his face lit up; as I am sure mine did too. It felt so good to see him. Whenever I did, I felt warm inside all over.

"Hey," Stuart said to me. "It's good to see you. I was just asking Peter if you all wanted to see the Northern Lights tonight on the lake. I read they're supposed to be spectacular and it looks like the skies will be clear too." I looked over at Peter who was ignoring my entrance.

"I think that would be great," I said.

"I can pick you guys up in my boat around nine then," Stuart said to both of us.

Peter looked up then. "I'll take my boat and pick you up. Claire will want to come too and my boat is bigger," he said.

"Ok, see you at nine then," Stuart squeezed my hand and left us.

I sat down next to Peter. "Peter, I'm sorry I didn't believe you were going to New York. Claire told me all about it, I think its great, and I wish you the best." I needed to get it off my chest, much like Karl needed to unload on me earlier; I felt it important that Peter know that I wished the best for him. He was after all, one of my best friends.

He looked at me then. "Thanks," was all he said. I could tell he did not want to apologize to me. I think he meant what he said to me earlier. Peter would always care about me and I knew that. He glanced over my shoulder. I looked back and there was Claire coming down to see us at the dock. She looked exhausted from her day at work.

"You got out late," I said.

"Yeah, well you missed the circus," she said as she plopped down on the dock. "Danielle showed up to find Dave, I told her he was not on the AM shift but she waited for him to show up. She seemed really anxious to talk to him. When he finally showed up, late, of course, he asked me to take over the bar for a few minutes while he spoke with her. They went out on the deck and started arguing about something, and the manager had to go out and ask her to leave the premises. Dave did not look at all happy when he came back into the bar. I actually felt sorry for him."

I listened with a tiny twist in the pit of my stomach. Something about Danielle did not bode well. She had issues that I didn't understand and she scared me. I wished she wasn't involved in Stuart's life.

Later we met at Peter's dock with blankets and a couple of bottles of wine. We got into his boat and headed over to collect Stuart. He was waiting for us on his dock, climbed in next to me and we took off for the cove where we could anchor the boat and watch the Northern Lights.

There is no easy way to describe the Northern Lights unless you have seen them for yourself. That night was the last time I saw them, although they appear periodically and sometimes the news will announce the coming attraction. The best time to see the Northern Lights — *Aurora Borealis*, as they are called in the Northern Hemisphere — is during the winter months, when the nights are longer. Unfortunately, this is also when people tend to stay inside more. Once in awhile, as was the case that summer, they make an appearance during the summer months. The Aurora Borealis is a light show from heaven, pulsing lights that ripple and race across the horizon in hues of green and purple. These strange colors are caused by the friction of sun particles colliding in the atmosphere. I imagine people that view them for the first time without knowing what they are might think there is a large fire somewhere off in the distance, or maybe an alien invasion of some sort.

We sat on the edge of the boat, drinking our wine, our feet dangling over the water, watching the light show in the sky. Finally, Claire decided it was time to jump in. She quickly tore off her clothes, and jumped into the glow of the lake. We all joined her. The water that night was the same temperature as the air. It was like swimming in nothingness. I looked over at Stuart and thought that since today was a day of confessions, tonight when I was alone with him. I would tell him how I felt, maybe even make love with him.

We got back in the boat laughing, and the two of us huddled under a blanket. I could feel his warm body and heart beating next to mine. We stayed this way until we pulled up to his dock. I was planning on disembarking with Stuart as well, but when we arrived, his father was waiting for us. He somberly grabbed the side of the boat as Peter docked it.

"Hey guys," he said. "Stuart, I have some bad news. Your cousin Danielle had an incident today and she's in the hospital. She's been asking for you."

We all went quiet. Stuart's mood changed immediately to one of concern. He left my side and climbed out of the boat to the dock next to his dad.

"Is she alright?" he asked.

"She'll be fine." His father looked at us, and waved. "Sorry to ruin your fun evening. Say hi to your folks, and your Aunt for me."

I was crestfallen; another chance to talk with Stuart gone, and I only had a few weeks left until I had to head back to college. When I got back to our camp Audrey was still awake, waiting for me on the screened porch. She had heard the news about Danielle.

"What's wrong with her?" I asked Audrey.

"I'm not sure Emalee. All I heard is that she had a mental breakdown of some sort earlier this evening and they took her to the psychiatric ward in the hospital."

"Has this happened before?"

"Well, for the past few years I know that she's had some trouble. I've heard from members of the Lowell family that she may be bipolar; they have been trying to figure it all out. She was always such a happy child. I remember her when she was younger. Her family used to come to the lake all the time, but then her father, Mark, got divorced a few years ago and they stopped coming for awhile. This is the first summer she's been here on her own at the family camp. She must be a bit lonely there all by herself. Mark only comes up on the weekends, and even then, not that often."

"Doesn't she have siblings?" I asked, wondering why the burden of taking care of her was falling on Stuart.

"She was adopted, and the only child they had. From what I hear, her depression and mood swings started after the divorce. But then you never know what triggers mental illness. Sometimes it hits people later in their life." She looked over at me with a stare that said, 'And we know this, don't we?' My mind was reeling from all of the revelations of the day, and the night swimming. I hit the bed and slept through until noon the next day. When I woke, I was hoping I would hear from Stuart, but I did not see him until the day before my departure for college.

He came by the camp to say good-bye. He knew I was leaving the next day and was apologetic about not seeing me since the night of the Northern Lights, but, he said, "I've been helping Danielle recover."

I didn't ask him what that meant, and I didn't want to talk about her on the last day I was with him before school. I took his hand.

"Come with me," I said. "I want to show you something cool."

I led him from our camp to the farmland across the road. There was an abandoned barn and remnants of the foundation of a house. The land was a field of Timothy-grass, being leased by some farmer for hay. It hadn't been mowed yet for harvest. We worked our way through the fields of grass mixed with milkweed to where the foundation of the house stood. There, in front of the foundation, in a big circle of uncut grass, was a field of *Coreopsis*, a perennial flower that blooms like sunshine. There were hundreds of them, as they had been left alone to propagate through the years, undisturbed by a gardener's hand thinning. I had discovered it a few weeks before and had been cutting and putting them in vases at the camp.

"Wow, look at this, it almost looks like someone left these for us to find, to remind us they lived here once," Stuart said. I laughed.

"Isn't it beautiful?" I said. We turned to look at each other. Again I saw that longing in his eyes, I wanted to cry. He held me then, embraced me, and we walked back to the camp.

"I have to go now," he said awkwardly. I hated him leaving me.

"I plan to come back in a few weeks," I said rapidly, "to help Audrey close the camp. Will you be around?" I was hoping, since he had graduated from college and was still working on his graduate school applications that maybe he'd be working at the marina this fall.

He brightened then. "Yes, I'll be around this fall," he said. 'Good', I thought. There is still time for me; still hope for us. It made saying good-bye a little less painful that day.

I also had to say farewell to Peter and Claire. They were

excited as ever about their move to New York. They were packing up Peter's things in her car that afternoon when I walked over to say good-bye and good luck to them both. Peter hugged me and wished me luck as well.

"I hope you find something you like to do in school," he said to me.

Audrey dropped me off at school but I lacked the anticipation and excitement I usually felt for the semester ahead. We were having an Indian summer that year and the temperatures were reaching into the high 80s through mid-September, which made it even harder for my friends and me to concentrate on studying. Every chance we got, my roommates and I would head for the college docks stationed at the edge of Seneca Lake. We would work our way down the steep cliff, navigate around the sailboats that were docked there for the sailing team, and jump in the cool lake waters, sunning ourselves on the docks until our next class. Showing up to class wet, with a bathing suit under our clothes, was not unusual for any of us that fall. Being in Seneca Lake, a vast, cold-water lake, only made me long for the camp on Canandaigua. I missed the camp and I missed Stuart. I had written him but he had not written me back. I didn't understand why. As I struggled to get through the weeks until the third weekend of September and my return to the camp, I kept vigil for the mail hoping to hear from him. I began to wonder if he would be in Canandaigua as he said he would.

The weekend finally came. I left early that Friday, Audrey picked me up and we headed right to the camp to begin the task of closing it up for the winter. It was an involved process of packing and putting away the sheets and towels and blankets; making sure the kitchen was devoid of any leftover food that might attract mice. Audrey instructed the plumber to come after we left to turn off the water and clear the pipes so they wouldn't freeze over the winter months. And we had to make sure that all of the storm windows were in place so that ice and snow did not seep through and cause water damage.

Audrey and I worked side by side all afternoon while I waited to hear from Stuart.

"Have you seen or heard from Stuart?" I asked her.

"Yes, I forgot to tell you. He came by yesterday looking for you, wondering when you would be back."

Forgot to tell me! I couldn't believe she waited so long. I was elated that he wanted to see me again. I quickened my pace to get the closing process over. I had to see Stuart, I had waited so long to see him. Everything was bottled up inside me, and I needed to get it all out. I didn't wait for Audrey to finish her chores. I biked over to his camp as soon as she said she didn't need me to help anymore.

When I arrived, Stuart was down at his docks working on his boat. He looked up at me and waved, a happy smile on his face. It was late by the time we sat down to the dinner he prepared for me. Around nine PM we went out on his deck so we could watch the harvest moon rising in the sky. The harvest moon is the full moon closest to the fall equinox, which happened to be that day, the first day of Autumn, one of the two days in the year, the other being in spring, when day and night are exactly twelve hours long. According to Native American tradition, people could work into the night to get the last of the corn harvest because the moon was so bright.

We sat on his deck looking out over the water. Stuart wrapped blankets around us to keep the chill off, and we drank wine while we watched the moon rise. We talked and talked about our future plans, or his really, because he had applied to a number of schools and was waiting to hear back from them. He told me about his cousin Danielle, and her illness, and how much she relied on him. I listened well into the night, watching the moon rise higher and higher.

When it was as high in the sky as it was going to go, I

looked at him levelly, "Stuart, I'm not sure what it is, but when I'm with you, I feel really good. I feel so warm inside and happy."

He looked away from me, at the water. "I think about you all the time as well," he said, deflecting my attention towards the view in front of us. "But it's not me that makes you feel so good, it's this place. Here everything is perfect, including us, we don't have to know each other's hurt or anger, we can just be. It's like a courtship that doesn't end."

That was not exactly the answer I was looking for. But at least he was acknowledging he had feelings for me. I had been so sure of my feelings, and of his feelings for me. Now I was confused. We didn't let this get between us however, as we talked well into the night, laughed at each other's ideas, and sat staring at the moon as it made its descent in the sky.

It was around four AM, just before the sun would rise, when we finally got up and went to his bedroom, both of us spent from talking. The room Stuart shared with his brother was standing still in time, a young boy's room. There were twin beds, separated by a nightstand, some old posters on the walls, and baseball paraphernalia. We looked at each other to determine what to do next. An awkward realization hit us that it would not be appropriate to sleep together in his sister's or parents' beds, and we were both too tired to do anything else but sleep at that point, so we climbed into the twin beds, still giddy from exhaustion, and although tired, continued talking until dawn. I must have fallen asleep at some point.

It was raining when I woke up and I could hear muffled voices downstairs. Stuart wasn't in his bed anymore. I tiptoed down the stairs leading to the kitchen and peeked over the rail to see him arguing with Danielle out on the deck. Danielle was pleading with him. Her hands were flailing wildly about her head as she tried to explain something to Stuart. He stood solidly in place, looking away from her, not saying anything. By now it was teeming. Her voice climbed an octave. She was screaming in the rain. In a gesture of desperation, she held his face between her hands, and kissed him hard on the lips. He responded at first, leaning into her body, making close contact with her. And then he took hold of her hands, brought them down to her side, and pushed her away. She looked at him, and fell into his arms. He embraced her as she collapsed, keening in anguish; over what, I did not know.

I couldn't stand to see this. I quietly left the house, got on my bike and pedaled as hard as I could in the rain. I was exhausted, drenched, and utterly confused by the time I got to my camp. I went straight to my room, took off my wet clothes, and went to bed. Audrey must have known something was wrong. She came in to check on me, at one point telling me Stuart was on the phone and wanted to talk with me. I would not get out of bed.

Finally, late Sunday morning, she came into my room and sat at the end of my bed.

"Emalee," she said, "I have some bad news. Danielle is dead."

I bolted upright. "What? Are you sure?"

"Yes," Audrey shook her head sadly. "Stuart found her last evening, at the end of her dock, under ten feet of water. According to the autopsy, she was four months pregnant. And they don't think her drowning was an accident."

- *Part Two Seneca* -

CHAPTER SEVEN

I always greet the turning of the autumn leaves with mixed emotion, for it signifies the winding down of that veritable energy cyclone which is summer in the Northeast.

— John A. Weeks

Missing the lake as I inevitably did when it was time to go back to school, I decided that fall to sign up for a class in Limnology: the study of freshwater lakes. Seneca Lake is an ideal place for limnological research. The lake is the largest and deepest of all of the eleven Finger Lakes. About twice as long, deep, and wide as Canandaigua, Seneca is forty miles long, three miles wide and 600-feet deep at its deepest point, although there is some debate about that. Indeed, the lake is so deep that the U.S. Navy operates a sonar-testing rig off shore in the middle of it. It also has a huge watershed — the land surrounding the lake that drains into it. I was especially thankful for the diversion this class gave me from my tumultuous feelings. Limnology also made me appreciate scientists' relentless pursuit of data.

A team of professors from various scientific disciplines

taught the class. They covered the physical, chemical and biological sciences of the lake system. Our labs were on Seneca Lake aboard the *William Scandling* research vessel: once a fishing boat, then a coast guard vessel, it was retrofitted for research.

Unlike land, lakes have nothing to intercept the wind. There are no buildings or trees getting in the way of a storm, so Seneca also has a large 'fetch', or surface area allowing wind to come spiraling down the lake. Periodically, when the winds generate in the south, the north end exhibits huge whitecaps, and wind surfing enthusiasts dive-bomb the waves. They come from all over the region, put on their wet suits, harness to their sails, foot-strap themselves to their boards, and head into the lake at the state park. They plane on the water, reaching great heights in the air.

This wave action also stirs up the lake sediments after heavy storms, causing the lake to become a brownish-green tinge from all of the sediments mixing throughout the water column. We could measure this turbidity with an instrument on the vessel called a secchi disk, a round black and white, oval-shaped instrument that is lowered into the water column until you can't see it anymore. The farther down it goes before it's not visible, the clearer the water that day.

Out on the research vessel we took water samples from all depths of the lake to measure the amount of oxygen found in the water — vital for all life — and the nutrient content, as well as the pH and temperatures. The vessel has a hydraulically powered boom and 1,500 feet of steel cable to bring water and sediment up from the depths below, which allowed us to collect sediments and samples of plankton, tiny microscopic animals that float in the lake at various depths.

My favorite lab was held at night. Our biology professor took us out to collect and quantify the presence of the ghost-like shrimp, *Mysis relicata.* This species of Mysid is one of the few that is adapted to freshwater. It's a relic of the glacial ages, and one theory is that the species migrated from ocean waters during the period when glaciers were scouring the lake basins. The females carry their brood of young in a pouch, hence the common name — opossum shrimp. They look like miniature crayfish under a microscope and have huge black eyes for seeing in the dark as they spend most of their time at the bottom of the lake. At night, they migrate to the upper reaches to feed on algae and other planktonic creatures that linger at the top of the water column. The dark night waters allow them to avoid predation from fish.

For this lab, we set out one cool fall evening in October and stationed ourselves just offshore from the campus. The steel cable forced the large plankton net down sixty feet into the dark water. What came up looked like tiny swimming ghosts. We put the samples in collecting bottles, labeling them with the date, time, and depth. We put them on ice, and recorded in our lab notebooks the water temperatures and oxygen content. Back in the laboratory we identified and counted the tiny organisms for our professor's continued research on the topic of migration patterns.

When the time came to decide if I wanted to sign up for a summer research stint in aquatic sciences at the college, I jumped on it. I applied to work with the biologists that spent their summers collecting from the lakes and streams in the Finger Lakes region. I was accepted into the program, and that allowed me to live on campus for the summer and receive a modest stipend. Audrey was happy I was accepted. She knew I did not want to come back to the camp that summer. During the winter break I had the chance to catch up with her and find out more about the aftermath of Danielle's drowning.

"Stuart and the family are devastated. She did not leave

a note," Audrey informed me over breakfast one morning during the break. It was a cold January morning. We were sitting at the breakfast nook in the kitchen, looking out the window at the gray and dreary day. I listened without asking any questions.

"You don't want to hear about all of this do you?" she asked and abruptly changed the subject. "You know, I was required to take a course in Greek mythology in college." She got up to take her teacup to the sink for a rinse. "And I remember this professor of mine, forget his name of course — old age." She glanced at me from the sink and smiled. "He was an odd bird alright. He would call us all by mythological Greek names such as Daedalus, Theseus, Icarus; I was Clytiё, the water nymph."

I perked up a bit and listened to her story; Audrey was a great story-teller. She rinsed her cup methodically, and placed it on the counter to drain.

"Clytiё lived in an ocean cave and was completely satisfied with the beauty of the sea around her, *until*," she emphasized with a wave of her hand, "she became enamored with Apollo, the Sun God. Unfortunately, Apollo had his sights on another, and took no interest in poor Clytiё. She was heartbroken of course, and spent days staring at the sun, hoping that Apollo would recognize her beauty." Audrey came over to the table and sat across from me. "After nine days the Fates took pity on her and turned her into a sunflower. To this day myth has it that sunflowers follow the sun because of their love." She watched me curiously with a look that I recognized. She was expecting me to ask her a question. She wanted a give and take.

I looked away. "What's the point?" I was in no mood to be her student.

"Oh, I don't know, it's just a silly myth. I looked it up of course once my professor assigned me the name. What do you think the meaning of the story is?"

"Well," I couldn't help but go along, "it sounds like she

was pining away for nothing. And she was wasting her time. Not very smart if you ask me."

"Yes," Audrey agreed, "indeed, she symbolized the longing in all of us for something we can't have." She patted my hand, got up from her chair, and left me in the kitchen.

There hadn't been much sun over the break, and the days were cold and wet. I spent a lot of the time holed up inside by the fire reading. The weather, combined with my mood, caused me to stay close to home. I had no motivation to see my old high school friends, Laurel included. She called me to ask how I was doing, but I did not want to get into a conversation with her about Stuart, and I knew she wanted to ask what had happened. The reality was, I was not sure what I could tell her anyway, as I hadn't heard from him since he tried to reach me the day after we watched the harvest moon rise and fall.

One night while we were building a fire, we talked about my summer plans. I admitted to Audrey that part of my motivation to stay on campus was to avoid the lake, and Stuart. Audrey filled me in on some details of his life after Danielle's death. He had gone back home after they scattered Danielle's ashes over the lake. He was applying to various schools and was waiting to hear from a university in Switzerland. She was hoping I would reveal what I knew about what happened.

"From what his mother tells me Stuart blames himself for Danielle's death," she said. "I guess they had some kind of argument earlier that day." She looked over at me. "You were with him the night before, did he say anything to you about Danielle's state of mind?"

I gazed at her, not quite listening. Then it struck me that maybe Audrey thought I knew more than she did. "Audrey," I answered, "I have no idea what was going on in Danielle's head."

Looking back on those dark days, I recall with

fondness Audrey's special quality of knowing my moods and not asking about my unwillingness to be social with my friends, or why I hadn't spoken with Stuart. She and I spent evenings talking about things such as her relationship with Karl, the future of the camp, and the costs of keeping it up. She recounted some of her memories of my father and the times they spent at the camp.

She talked a lot about Karl. "He and I always had a thing for each other, but when his family sold the camp I just assumed it was over. I couldn't believe it when I ran into him again after all of those years. It was like we never lost touch with each other; we simply took up where we left off," she said. "I never felt guilty about it, but I know it bothered Karl. He would come see me after a particularly grueling time with his wife's cancer treatment and we would sit quietly at the lake. It was a chance for him to regain his strength so he could be there for her."

I pictured how this must have been for both of them, a chance to reconnect, the solitude of the lake, and then I arrived on the scene. It was a testament to their relationship that they were able to deal with absence, time, death of loved ones, and then me, a teenager who had just lost her parents in a tragic murder/suicide. Other people might have given up on each other, let go. How many people remain friends or lovers when adversity gets in their way?

CHAPTER EIGHT

Mayfly nymphs live in clean, fresh waters, flowing rivulets, or rivers, tumbling waterfalls or quiet pools; they have become adapted to every aquatic situation except foul water. – Ann Haven Morgan

That summer I was assigned to work with a retired professor at the university. She was a stream ecologist, and had spent her professional life studying the aquatic organisms that inhabit streams. I had never met her before, but she had a reputation for being a hard-working and sometimes demanding supervisor.

I first encountered Dr. Martha, as everyone called her, waiting in the lab with fellow students for our instructions. She breezed in to collect a few items, glanced over at us all, waved, and then breezed back out. She hardly looked her seventy-five years. At about the same time, an auburn-haired student came into the lab and asked us to quiet down so he could orient us to the summer research program, lab procedures, and safety. His name was Toby Smith, a sophomore, who, from what I heard, was a favorite of all the biology department professors. I recognized him from my fall limnology class. It seemed to me he was somewhat nonchalant about safety.

He proceeded to lead us down to the closet that held all of the outdoor gear, rubber waders, boots, raincoats, and nets. "This is the stream studies equipment room," he said to us. I looked through the gear to find my size; I knew that working with Dr. Martha would mean wading into streams sometimes past my waist and that I would need the waders.

We followed him to the aquatic labs. A window decal on the door said 'Have you hugged a limnologist today?' The lab housed aquariums, microscopes, centrifuges and a spectrophotometer.

"You will be using all of this equipment at various times depending on who you are working with from week to week. Those of you working with Dr. Martha, follow me." He led a group of us down the hall to a large lab with microscopes, buckets and many vials neatly labeled with the names of the aquatic insects recently collected at stream sites. "You're gonna love working with Dr. Martha; she's the best," he said.

The other students and I looked at each other, barely suppressing a laugh. Toby's description of everything so far had been 'the best' this or 'the best' that. People were 'the best,' places in town to eat or drink were 'the best.' If we believed him, the world was full of nothing but the best. I could understand why the professors liked him; his enthusiasm was endearing.

When we broke to take off for lunch he came up to me. "Emalee Rawlings, right?" He followed me out the door, "So I understand you're working with Dr. Martha," he said, walking along beside me.

"Yes, mostly," I answered, "although I think I may be doing some lake studies as well with Professor Warner." I was surprised that he took any notice of me.

"Well, you will only want to work with Dr. Martha once you get started. She can be demanding you know, but she is always interesting."

"How would you know?" I asked him. His know-it-all attitude was starting to get on my nerves.

"I worked with her this past spring as an assistant. She has so much clout around here she always has a student or two working with her. She's a favorite of the administration and it drives the other faculty crazy. She's famous, you know. She has published all kinds of papers and even wrote a book about aquatic insects and their habitats."

I stopped walking then and looked this young, earnest man over. He was trying to impress me, I could tell. He stopped and looked me in the eyes with an expression that said, 'What? You don't believe me?' I took him to be about nineteen, a year or two younger than me. He had a boyish air about him, his hair was unruly, even his clothes looked unkempt, as if he didn't do laundry until he had no other choice.

"How do you know me?" I asked him, realizing he knew my name.

"I remember you from Limnology," he smiled brightly at me.

"Look, I appreciate you showing me the ropes and all, but I'd like to form my own opinion about Dr. Martha. I've gotta go now and eat something, maybe I'll see you later?" I said to him. But he wouldn't be put off.

"I have to eat too, want to get some lunch with me?" he asked.

"Not today. Maybe another time," I said. I almost felt sorry for him when I saw his expression change from one of anticipation to disappointment. Was he serious?

"OK," he shrugged. "I'll see you later this afternoon then."

"Wait; what?" I asked.

"I'm working with Dr. Martha this summer too," he shouted, walking backwards towards the dining hall.

That afternoon we sat sweating in the lab, waiting for Dr.

Martha. The heat and humidity was unbearable. The air was so close, even sweat could not evaporate from the skin. I couldn't wait to get out of the lab and into a stream or lake.

Dr. Martha strolled in and glanced around at her summer crew. She smiled when her gaze landed on Toby. "Well thanks for coming in this heat! I know you would all rather be in the lake swimming or something more fun than listening to an old lady talk about bugs!"

She had our attention. She reached for a textbook on the shelf and slammed it down on the lab table; it was titled *Freshwater Invertebrates of the United States* by Robert Pennak.

"This," she said, "will be your bible for the summer. Every insect you collect from the streams will be in here, or they have never been found, and I doubt you will be the first to discover a new insect species. You'll need to follow and understand the keys in this guide so that you can identify the insects down to the family," she told us.

I was perspiring and wishing that there was more air circulation in the room. Sweat ran down my forehead and into my eyes. Blinking away the sweat, I looked around at the other students, steaming up as well; except for Toby, who was ignoring the lecture and fidgeting with a microscope lens.

On the tables were large buckets labeled with the date, time and the name of the creek from which the contents were collected. They were filled with small amounts of stream water, preservative, sediment and decaying matter, and in the muck and vegetative debris were aquatic insects. We spent the rest of the afternoon teasing the insects out of the mud and debris. I lifted a lacey remnant of a decaying maple leaf to find a dead insect still clinging to it. From my observation the insect had done quite a number on it, as the only thing left to eat were the fine veins that carry water and nutrients. It looked like the outline of a stained glass window waiting for the glass.

"You will find that certain segments of streams favor particular species of aquatic insects depending on the vegetation present," Dr. Martha appeared out of nowhere.

I was so intrigued by the leaf I hadn't noticed her presence.

We plunked the insects into white tin pans of water so that we could more easily identify them. First we had to determine whether they were a pupa or a nymph. If they had legs, we had to see if they were jointed or not, and look for claws. We had to find their gills and look for their placement on the segmented bodies. This could be tricky, and Dr. Martha was vigilant in making sure we did not make assumptions.

Evelyn, one of the students working on our team, was about to label an insect in a vial a 'stonefly' when Dr. Martha asked, "How did you come to that conclusion?"

Evelyn blushed, worried she had it wrong. "Well, there are two tails. The key says if it has two tails it's probably a stonefly," she answered.

"Yes, that could be, but what else does the key say?" Dr. Martha asked, pointing at the key. They both looked.

Evelyn's face lit up with sudden acknowledgement. "Oh, I need to look at the location of the gills."

She seemed relieved to have been able to figure it out on her own without Dr. Martha telling her the answer. She took the insect out of the vial, placed it on the table and examined it under a magnifying lens. Stoneflies and some mayfly species have two tails; one way to differentiate them is the location of their gills. On mayfly they are located along the abdomen. Evelyn had a mayfly.

There were so many new words and terms to decipher in the key that my head was spinning by the end of the day. Toby surprised me with his quick knowledge of the terms, and his ability to help students interpret what they were looking at under the microscopes using the Pennak key. He obviously had spent some time with this textbook.

When it was time to go, he studiously went around the room to make sure we had identified the insects correctly, and showed us Dr. Martha's preferred way of labeling the specimens.

I wasn't at all surprised when he came up to me as I was trying to leave and asked me to go out with him to a local bar that night.

"Aren't you under-age?" I asked him, hoping my air of superiority would throw him off.

"Who isn't around here?" he said in reply. He had a point, everyone on campus found a way to drink at the local bars, using fake or borrowed i.d.

"I don't think so Toby. I'm really beat. Maybe another time," I told him. He was not deterred.

"Ok, great then, let's shoot for tomorrow night. We can have dinner first. I know of a cheap restaurant in town that's the best."

I laughed then, because I was so exhausted and he was so determined to take me out. I relented. "OK, I'll go with you tomorrow."

Toby came to my house around six and we walked to the local restaurant. It was not exactly 'the best' I had ever eaten, but the air conditioning felt good. Toby ate voraciously, as if it was his last meal before a fast.

"So, I don't know if you remember me from Limnology, but I had a pony-tail back then," he said in between bites. It was interesting to watch him eat. He barely took the time to come up for air. He had his salad eaten before I even started on mine.

"Oh yes, I remember you now. I really liked that class and the professors," I said. "I don't remember working with you as a lab partner at all though, so I'm surprised you remember me."

He looked up from his plate. "I remember you always looked sad, especially when we were on the research vessel. You were always staring out at the lake with this lost look," he said.

Well, he was perceptive; I admired that.

He pointed his fork at me. "But I always liked your eyes, you have great eyelashes," he said.

I laughed at that, eyelashes: eyelashes? What kind of pick up line was that? But he was sincere, and his intensity was disconcerting. I had to look away from him to keep from laughing. "Thanks," I said, "no one has ever told me that before. So you like aquatic sciences?"

"Oh, I don't know, it seems better than the pre-med coursework I was taking, which required a lot of time sitting in the lab looking under a microscope and bacteria and parasites, and viruses and things I could never identify," he said. "But I don't plan to stick with biology once I graduate."

"Really, so what are your plans then?" I asked.

He looked up at me with that boyish grin he had, "I want to be an actor."

'Oh my God.' I thought, another Peter.

We spent the rest of the meal talking about Dr. Martha, his mentor, and the other professors we would be working with over the summer.

Toby explained the methods we would be using the next day to collect the aquatic insects. "Bring bug spray. The mosquitoes have been brutal so far this summer," he said.

He walked me home and insisted on coming in to see the house I was renting. I brought him to the kitchen and we had a beer at the table. Toby would not leave my house until well past midnight, so I got to bed late. Even then I was tossing and turning, as the only relief I had from the heat was a small plastic fan blowing the humid air around the room.

Our first destination was Kashong Creek, at the mouth, where it enters the lake. It was early morning and the air was still cool. The creek was swollen from the unrelenting rain we were experiencing that June. Dr. Martha forded the stream with considerable agility. She showed us her methods for collecting the insects.

"Find a place in the creek where there is an obvious riffle, where the water is rippling over stones or boulders. Then spread out in groups of two, and start collecting samples along a transect across the creek," she said as Toby demonstrated by standing diagonal to Dr. Martha towards the other side of the creek. "Come here Emalee," she motioned to me to stand by her, "and bring one of those nets with you." I grabbed a net and she waved Toby over.

"Now we do what is called the 'riffle dance,' she smiled. "As Toby stands directly in front of Emalee with his net flat against the bottom of the creek bed, Emalee will twist and turn, churning up the water and rocks to dislodge the aquatic insects living in the sediments." I began twisting my old sneakers in the gravelly bottom the way she showed me.

"No, Emalee, you are not putting enough into it." She gently pushed me out of the way and swished her boots back and forth in a violent motion that stirred the sediments up and sent them careening towards Toby's waiting net. "Like this!" Once again her energy surprised me.

She handed us all waterproof notebooks and told us to record the size of the rocks and pebbles we found, the water temperature, the stream velocity, and the dissolved oxygen levels. She emphasized the importance of also recording the type of land around the stream site. Was it forested, fields, or urban? We were to take note of the types of trees we saw, and if we could not identify them, take a sample twig and leaf back to identify later. However she knew a lot of the trees, and would tell us what we were looking at if we didn't know. We divided into teams of three and went to work.

I couldn't help but notice Toby while we worked; he

was bouncing around the stream like a puppy. While Dr. Martha sat along the shoreline watching our technique and shouting out instructions, he was chatting it up with all of the students, especially the co-eds. He would point to things we found in our nets and tell us what they were, and help place the samples into plastic containers, then pour a solution of ethanol in to preserve the specimens, while we moved along the transect line. Every once in awhile he would bring something over to Dr. Martha to have her identify it.

I sifted through my net looking for insects and put a few in a small tray to observe before putting the contents in a container. A creature caught my eye, pumping away in the water to form a current over its feathery gills. I took out my notebook to make a drawing of the thing so that I could remember to identify it when we got back to the lab.

"That is the burrowing mayfly," Dr. Martha breathed in my ear. I stiffened in place, as I could not figure how she reached me in the stream so quickly from her perch along the edge. "It's probably the genus *Hexagenia.* They're usually found along the lake shoreline and in slower moving streams," she said. "This mayfly creates huge swarms over the lake and near lights. It sometimes scares people who are not sure what they are, you see. It was once extirpated from the Lake Erie Basin until it made a comeback in the early 1990s. Very sensitive to pollution," she mused. I was not sure what 'extirpated' meant, but I assumed it was bad; later I found out it means to be extinct in a particular location, but not everywhere.

We finally finished at this site and moved upstream to another station. Toby was right about the mosquitoes; they were relentless. By late morning, every movement was an exertion, the air becoming so dense we were swimming in it. All of us were starting to wither in the heat. Remarkably, Dr. Martha continued moving along at quite a clip. She and Toby were ahead of us, scouting out the next site. As we traversed the creek bed, we could hear each other clomping on the rock and broken shale, each step a balancing act. We never knew when a rock would upend from our weight and send us tumbling into the creek. Everyone was stewing in their own thoughts. The only sounds were of rocks lifting then falling, clunking back in place and light dripping as the leaves let loose the rain that had been adhering to them since the rainfall the night before. The ravine became narrower and the overhanging trees provided some respite from the beating sun as we walked upstream. There were visible pools of water, formed where the stream had eroded away at the rocks and shale, which looked really inviting to wade in.

We followed the same protocols, but this time we also took samples from the pools. Everyone put on waders. Evelyn was the first to venture in. It was hard to gauge the depth of the water. She took a meter stick with her, waded in, stumbled, and found herself over waist-deep in the pool with water flooding her waders. She screamed, then laughed, and we all laughed with her. She came out soaked, kicked off the waders, and grabbed her sneakers out of her backpack.

I envied her then, having more freedom without the waders on to tramp about the water. Indeed, the waders were making me sweat; they were heavy and covered the entire lower half of my body. I decided to take mine off as well, and soon everyone followed suit with a collective sigh of relief. We left the waders along the side of the creek to collect on our way back after the final station upstream. Tramping through the cool, clean water of Kashong Creek was just what we needed — a respite from the oppressive heat and humidity.

The more we worked our way upstream, the deeper the ravine became, and the swifter the water. Toby started to assist Dr. Martha navigate the rocks and boulders we encountered along the way.

At the next, and final site, he came up to me. "There is a great waterfall further up from here. Someday I will show you," he said.

I knew places like this in Canandaigua. We would troll the lakeshore looking for these cool glens, anchor our boats, and wade into them looking for waterfalls with plunging pools at the bottom. The pools were ice cold, the water source springs that reside in the upper reaches. Like most of the geography of the Finger Lakes, these waterfalls were formed by glacial activity. As the climate changed, and the glaciers melted and receded northward thousands of years ago, they forced the tributaries leading into the engorged river valleys back. With exertion and force, the glaciers caused the streams to dislocate from their floors, creating gorges in places along the east and west sides of the Finger Lakes. Thinking of the glens made me homesick for the camp.

We finally finished our last sampling for the day, and just in time for the rain to come. We quickly took out our rain gear and slogged our way back to the waiting van. It was slow going for most of us, but harder on Dr. Martha. Toby remained by her side making sure she didn't trip and stumble over the rocks. We quickly loaded the equipment, waders, and samples into the van and Toby drove us back to campus. As soon as we arrived, Dr. Martha got out, waved good-bye to us, got into her own car, and drove off. We were left to unload and put the samples in the lab to identify and label the next day.

When we finished I got out of there, headed home, and took a quick shower to wash off all the scum and rotting vegetation from my legs and feet. I grabbed a sandwich and told my housemates that I was going to bed and not to disturb me for anything. I laid my head on my pillow, the sheets damp from the humidity. Everything felt damp and cool, much like the ravine I had been in all day.

I didn't care, I was asleep within minutes.

Very few labs or offices in the science building we were

working in had air conditioning back then. It was sweltering in the lab; the few fans placed in the room were circulating steamy air. We repeated the procedures of identifying, labeling, and putting our specimens in vials for later reference. We also had to transfer our notes to lab sheets provided by Toby. I wondered how long the insects lasted in these vials of preservative. I asked Toby.

"Come with me," he said. He took me to Dr. Martha's office. She had not shown up at the labs yet, and she was not in her office either. Toby had the key. We entered the small, air-conditioned office. It was crowded with stacks of lab sheets and notebooks from years past. Her shelves were full of books. I went over the shelves and took one of the smaller, older books out. It was titled *Field Book of Ponds and Streams* by Ann Haven Morgan, written in 1930. It was a small, old, charming book filled with sketches and colored pictures of the same insects we were identifying in the labs. But the descriptions of the insects and other aquatic creatures were more interesting, less technical than Pennak's text.

"That was my textbook in college." Dr. Martha entered the room. I jumped. I still could not get used to her ability to appear out of nowhere.

"I had the privilege to study under Dr. Morgan. She reluctantly took me on as her student, the last before she retired from Mt. Holyoke College," she continued.

"What a lovely book," I said.

"Yes, she was a pioneer in her time. She understood these aquatic creatures like no other person. She was nicknamed 'Mayfly Morgan' by her peers, and anglers used her sketches to make their ties for catching trout," she explained.

I looked at other books on her shelf. There were a few written by Emerson Klees on the history of the Finger Lakes and a book called *Aquatic Insects of the Finger Lakes: A Natural History* by Dr. Martha Prescott. I looked over at Toby, he was playing around with the vials of specimens on another shelf and he almost dropped one, juggled it in the air, then placed it back.

"Toby, be more careful with those," Dr. Martha scolded. Toby was unfazed as he went over to her computer to turn it on. I began to think he had Attention Deficit Disorder, and that maybe it was rubbing off on me, as I could not recall why we had come to Dr. Martha's office, and she hadn't asked.

She turned back to me. "You can take that home if you like," she said to me while I was leafing through her book.

I looked up, "That would be great," I said.

"You need a new computer," Toby interrupted.

Dr. Martha frowned. "I don't want a new computer — I want you to fix that one," she said to him.

"Can't do it: it's time to move on. You need a computer with new operating software if you want to use the latest database system, otherwise it won't work," he told her.

She sighed. "Well, we will just have to find someone to input the data for me on another computer system, because I am not upgrading. Now please excuse me so I can get some work done," she told us both irritably.

"Boy she is in a bad mood today," Toby said as we were leaving her office. "Must be the heat."

When we got back to the lab he asked everyone if they wanted to meet later that night for pizza. The idea of eating in an air-conditioned restaurant was too good to pass up: we all met up at our favorite pizza joint.

At the restaurant, two of the coeds on our team immediately found a seat at the table nearest Toby; it was so predictable. He sat there chatting it up with them, every once in awhile stealing a glance my way. I tried to ignore him. I was engaged in a conversation with one of the other students about a study abroad program in Australia. It sounded like fun. When dinner was over and we were walking home, Toby came up and started walking along beside me.

"What's up with Dr. Martha's pile of papers on her desk?" I asked him while walking.

"That's all of her unpublished data," he said. "She has about 15 years' worth of those data sheets and student notebooks sitting there, waiting to be put into a database so that she, or someone, can make some sense of it."

"And you haven't volunteered yet?" I asked, amused, everyone knew Toby was her favorite, a teacher's pet.

He looked at me with a serious stare, "Nope, she hasn't asked me," he said. "I don't think just anyone is going to be doing that job for her."

I was so relieved the next day, when Dr. Warner came in and asked for volunteers to go with him on the research vessel the following morning. The tedious nature of sifting through rotting vegetation looking for insects was starting to get on my nerves, and the lack of air conditioning amongst the smells was making me dizzy. I didn't think I could take another day of it and we still had six weeks of summer to go. I raised my hand to volunteer, and then, much to my chagrin, so did Toby. I had hoped to get away from his annoying banter for at least one day.

We took off from the docks at first sign of dawn because the weather forecast was predicting thunderstorms later in the day. One would hardly guess that bad weather was in the forecast given the still air. When we took off, the lake was calm. It would take an hour to reach the station mid-way down the lake because the sixty-five foot vessel did not move fast.

When we finally arrived, we drifted in place and started our collections following Dr. Warner's procedures. He had us run the plankton net — used to collect microscopic organisms — over the side of the hull and drag it a few times along the length of the boat. We took a small droplet of the sample and put it under the microscopes in the cabin just to see what algae were blooming. The slide was full of diatoms like the tube-shaped, *Fragillaria* and, my favorite the star-shaped diatom, *Asterionella.* These planktonic organisms are opportunists, taking advantage of the nutrients in the lake when they are at a maximum, which is usually in the late spring to early summer. They contain chloroplasts which allow them to photosynthesize, and are the base of the food chain for the lake, much like our plants.

The waves were picking up on the lake and the vessel started to pitch back and forth. After a while, looking under the microscope made me nauseous. I stepped out on the deck for air. All of those years of being on boats and I had never felt seasick before, but this lake was different. I looked out at the water. The wind was picking up from the south-west and the waves were white caps. I felt like I was in the ocean, they were so big. I also felt like I was going to vomit. Toby came out of the cabin to see if I was ok.

"You all right?" he asked. I shook my head, and threw-up over the side of the boat. He ran back into the cabin and brought me a wet cloth. "Here," he said, as he placed it on my forehead. "You need to keep your eyes on the horizon. You should be good at that." He winked at me. A thought passed my mind in that instant: although he could be annoying, Toby was kind.

I worked my way with his help to the back of the boat, and tried to keep my focus on the horizon. It wasn't helping much but I kept at it. Just then another student came out to see us.

"We are turning around and heading back, the storm is coming fast down the lake," he said, with a look of pity in his eyes as he glanced my way.

The boat slowly turned north, towards the home dock. I looked up to see a wall of black clouds in the south, heading in our direction. The wind was picking up, and there were flashes of lightning in the skies to the south.

We watched, with quiet fascination, the rain racing towards us. This storm was moving very fast. We were so caught up in the sight of it, we barely had time to get in the cabin and escape the torrential downpour.

Toby walked me back to my house in the rain.

"Thank you Toby," I said.

"No problem, that's happened to me before," he said. "Can I see you tonight?"

I still did not feel so well, and the thought of trying to be cheerful just exhausted me. But when I looked at him, I knew I had to throw him a bone.

"Not tonight, but maybe tomorrow?" I said.

"Great!" he exclaimed. "We can take a swim if it's hot." And he left me with a spring in his step.

He walked over to get me the next night and told me, "Put on a bathing suit, we are gonna go swimming."

'Night swimming; how romantic,' I thought. If only I was with someone else. I pulled on my suit, grabbed a towel, and we walked down the steep path that led to the lake. The campus docks were great during the day, but the campus security patrolled them at night. So we turned onto the railroad tracks that bordered the lakefront and headed to an abandoned beach-front with a small dock in the water. We were not the only ones with this idea. There were a few students swimming and others sitting on the dock when we got there. I did not recognize them. They must have been working with faculty from other departments, but Toby knew them all, of course, and sat down to tell them about his research on the lake on the infamous *William Scandling*. I began to think his calling was in politics, not acting. While he was busy being the ambassador of the lake, I waded in from the shore.

I had learned by then not to jump from the dock at night. Not when I couldn't tell what was in the water below. There was a half moon casting a pale light in the sky and the water appeared ink-black. I could not see the bottom. I knew from experience the things that might lurk at the bottom of a lake, segments of fallen trees, their limbs whittled down by the current into lances that could impale. If not tree limbs then the zebra mussels were enough to keep me from jumping. There was always the chance of getting cut by a zebra mussel. It had happened to me plenty of times on Canandaigua Lake. These mussels colonize on hard surfaces under water and have razor sharp sides, which could slice your feet. Getting cut by one of these little monsters was like a paper cut gone bad, it would last for weeks and every step would hurt. As I waded in safely from shore, I felt the scratchy carpet of *Chara*, an underwater alga that attaches itself to the bottom of the lake, under my feet. The water was cold. It would take a while to warm up, but the chill felt good.

We stayed late on the dock, talking with the other students and swimming. Toby knew some of them from the spring play production he had a part in. After a while everyone left except Toby and me. We were lying on the dock, looking up at the stars. I did not mind staying up late — the cool breezes off the lake felt good compared to my stuffy room back at the house.

As we lay there, Toby sat up and looked down at me, leaned over, took my head in his hand and kissed me on the lips. I felt a jolt of blood rush through my skin at his touch. He then softly, carefully, caressed every part of my body. I was vulnerable to his touch, he had been pursuing me all summer and I finally gave in to him. All of my pent up desire and longing, came pouring out at that moment. I hadn't realized how desperate I was for human connection. The next thing I knew he had removed my bathing suit, and was gently entering me. We enjoyed each other's cool, damp body as we made love on the docks. When it was over we lay back and looked up at the stars. I grabbed my towel and put it over me as I was feeling a bit exposed without his warm body on top of mine.

"That was the best," he said as he sighed heavily.

'The best?' Couldn't he have found a better description than to compare me to his favorite restaurant? He reached for my hand as we lay there side by side.

"I want to thank you," he said to me then.

"Thank me for what?"

He sat up, looked over at me. "For being my first."

"What do you mean, your first?"

"I mean, I was a virgin until tonight."

I couldn't believe it. I had no idea that I was going to be his pilot run, and wasn't sure I wanted the honor.

"Well," he said, lying back down on the dock, "it's not like I didn't have the chance with other women, believe me."

I looked over at him, lying there on his back looking up at the sky, with his tousled hair, bright smile, and sparkling eyes, and I believed him. "It's just that there was no challenge involved." He rolled over onto his side to look down at me then. "You are like a puzzle that I have been trying to piece together since I met you," he said.

I rolled on my side to face him, "Toby, you really should have warned me, and you never even asked me if I was on birth control." I couldn't believe I was giving a lecture about birth control, when just a year before I barely knew what it was. My towel came off and I saw him look down at my breasts with desire. I felt a chill, and grabbed the towel to cover up.

"It's time to go," I said, putting on my bathing suit. We walked down the tracks to the steep path leading back up towards campus and my house.

He followed me. "Jeez, I didn't think you would be mad at me about this. You seemed to enjoy it as much as I did," he said. I turned to him; he looked hurt.

"I just need to get home now Toby. Would you just walk me home?" I said.

CHAPTER NINE

Even some committed naturalists have difficulty remembering what things were like yesterday, let alone last year or in the last decade. If our perception of change is this weak, we are not likely to give much thought to the implications of change. — John A. Weeks

Lying in my bed that night with the fan blowing hot air in my face I looked up at the ceiling and could only think of one thing: Stuart. I had had a dream about him the other night. We embraced because we were so happy to see each other. I am sure the dream was instigated by a letter he had sent me earlier that week; I took it out to read it again.

Dear Emalee,

I hope all is going well with you and your research. Your Aunt told me you were working with scientists who study the lake and the streams. I'm sure you will enjoy the work; it may be your calling. I'm not sure if she told you but I am in Switzerland, I got a scholarship to a university in Geneva and am spending my summer here taking a few courses before my program begins in the fall. I am really excited, and I love this city!

It has been hard for me to write to you because I am still grieving

Danielle. It hit my family really hard. I think we all feel a bit responsible, as if maybe there was more we could have done to help her deal with her mental illness. I'm not sure how much your Aunt told you about what happened, and I don't want to relay it all in this letter, but the past several months have been hell for my family and me.

There is so much I want to say to you about last summer. I loved the time we spent together. It meant so much to me. But I was also conflicted because of my relationship with Danielle, which was very complicated. We grew up together and always looked out for one another, but Danielle became obsessed with me and let's just say it went too far. Even today I feel so much remorse about letting my relationship with her cross a line it should never have. In the end, I could not be a man to you both. I'm sorry you had to witness us arguing that morning. But I wish you hadn't left. There was so much I wanted to tell you. I hope one day we see each other again. Take care.

Love Stuart

His letter told me some of what I wanted to know, but it left a lot out. Like, what happened to Danielle that evening on the dock? Did she intentionally kill herself, and if so how? The lake was not that dangerously cold. I was in it over that weekend. We had had a warm fall and the water was still warm enough to swim. It would take a long time for a person to get hypothermia and drown, and Danielle was a strong swimmer. A twisted thought entered my mind: maybe Stuart killed her. Maybe he was on the dock with her that evening and shoved her out of anger. He left, assuming she would swim back to the dock but instead, she panicked and drowned. And what about the pregnancy? Stuart fails to mention it although he alludes to his relationship as going too far. Did that mean he got her pregnant, and when she realized he did not want to be a father she killed herself?

I couldn't sleep with all of these thoughts racing through my head. I put the letter away in my drawer and went to the kitchen to get a glass of milk. It was raining again, and I went outside to sit on the porch and get some fresh air. I sat in the rocking chair and looked out at the street-lights casting a depressing, pale glow on the sidewalks. What I missed the most, I realized, was not only the way Stuart and I were so happy when we were together, but also the way we responded to each other intellectually. I never felt vulnerable about getting too 'deep' with him, because he was a deep person himself. The two of us really opened up to each other and I loved that about him. That was why his relationship with Danielle was so confusing to me. What was he hiding?

And then I thought about Toby. What would happen with our friendship now that we had sex? I wished it hadn't happened although I realized how much I was longing for companionship. In spite of his faults, he was a good person. I didn't think he would be embarrassed or try to avoid me after that night. Little did I know how right I was.

In fact, after that night on the docks, Toby would not leave me alone. He glommed onto me like glue to paper. Even in the lab, I could feel his presence next to me all the time. He could be ten feet away and there was an electric current between us, a force pulling us together. I could not shake him or the force. He walked me home every day, sometimes coming in so that we could make love. He would leave me spent, longing for the next time we could be together. For a neophyte he was quite adept at love-making. His stamina was starting to wear on me though, and by the end of the week, I needed a break.

Dr. Martha called me into her office one day before the weekend. She said she wanted to show me something. Toby tried to follow along as usual and she waved him off. "I need to talk to Emalee, alone." When we got to her office I was worried that she was going to say something about my relationship with Toby. She was a keen observer. Had she noticed the electricity between us as well?

"Come over here Emalee; I want to show you something," she said, as we worked our way around her piles of papers and books strewn across the floor and any flat object in the small space of her office. "I want you to take a look at these notebooks, and tell me what you see."

I looked at the pile of notebooks, all similar to the ones we were using this summer in the field. I leafed through a few of them and noticed how very different their style was depending on the student. Some had made an effort to make detailed notes, drawn sketches, while other students made simple cursory remarks. I could also see where Dr. Martha had added some comments of her own, especially in the notebooks where a student had added thorough notes. I said as much after glancing through about ten of the notebooks.

"Yes. I find that some students are better at taking notes that others. Do you know why?" she asked me.

"No; I'm not sure," I did not know where she was leading.

"Well, some students have a knack for observing things that others miss. This is a skill I think you have. I have watched you in the field. You take the time to observe and jot down observations, while others have moved on to the next thing. I need someone like you to transcribe these notes, and the raw data I have, into a database system," she said.

I must have looked shocked, if not overwhelmed by her request.

"Don't worry, I will pay," she said.

"It's not that," I said, "I am sure it would be a worthwhile project, but there is at least 15 years of data here; it would take a long time to get through it, and why not ask Toby?" With all of the work he was doing for her it seemed reasonable that he would be her first pick for this job.

"Toby has boundless energy but he does not have the patience for this type of work. He would miss too many details, and I need someone who can make sense of all of this data. There is something there, I know it instinctively, but we need to quantify it, pinpoint it, tease a hypothesis out of all of this material," she told me.

I walked home that evening with a stack of the notebooks and copies of the data sheets, as well as a new laptop computer that housed the database system Dr. Martha wanted me to use to input the data. This could be a lifetime project, I thought. How was someone like me, who had a cursory understanding of stream biology, to make sense of these data? And why would she trust me, out of all of her students, to decipher any meanings from the notes? When I got home I started by looking through all of the notebooks. I could see where she had read some of the notes taken by the more observant students, and added comments in the margins like, 'construction site along creek bed, roots of trees and shrubs being smothered by construction material and heavy equipment.' Sure enough, when I found notes taken at the same site a few years later, she had written in the margins of one student's notes, 'most shrubs now gone, several trees dead, one large oak and willow under stress, new parking lot next to stream site, loss of shade.' These were her observations, put in the margins, as reminders of the change occurring at one of the sites she came back to every season. I wondered then if the data from this site would show a change in stream temperature over time due to the loss of shade?

I needed a strategy to tackle this project. I started with the stream site that ran through the City of Geneva – Castle Creek. This was the stream that did not have any mayflies present. Since Dr. Martha told us that mayflies were like canaries in a coal-mine (an idiom that went over my head until someone explained that caged canaries were brought into coal mines by the miners to test for lethal gases. If they died, it was a sure sign that things were not safe in the mine). The absence of mayflies would indicate that the water was polluted and would at least give me something to look for in the reams of notes and data. I began examining the notebooks that night.

The next day Toby wanted to follow me home again. I looked at him with mixed emotions. As much as I wished to spend time with him it seemed I had created a monster. All he wanted to do now was have sex. I needed a break. If I was ever to get anywhere with this data I could not spend as much time with him.

"Toby, I'm so tired, and I need to work on this project that Dr. Martha gave me to do," I said to him.

Again, I realized, he was not one for a brush-off. "OK. I will come by later tonight then. See you in a couple of hours," he said. And before I could protest, he was running back to his dorm.

He showed up at that night after I had eaten. I had all of the windows open to catch the cool, strong breeze coming in from the lake. The weather had finally broken and the days were clear and sunny, the nights cool and less humid. I could sleep without a fan now, and I found myself sleeping soundly, after exhausting days in the field, lab and then Toby. He came in and plopped down on the couch in front of me while I was working on the database.

"She finally got a laptop, huh?" he said alluding to Dr. Martha and the computer I was working on.

"Yes, and this is a lot of work, so please find something else to do for awhile. I'm busy," I said, annoyed at his presence. He walked over and put his arms around me, kissing my neck.

I wriggled away from him. "Toby, I'm serious. You need to leave me alone for a bit so I can finish this season's worth of data, and I haven't even gotten to transcribing the notes." He picked up the notebooks from the table, and glanced at the datasheets, sitting there waiting to be input into the database, stacked as high as my shoulders.

"I can help you," he said. I looked at him.

"Really?" I didn't think he would take an interest.

"Yes. If it means I can spend time with you, then yes," he said, "I don't know what else to do with myself." He smiled at me with that boyish grin that I hated and loved at the same time.

And so we struck a bargain that summer, Toby and I. I would spend time with him if he would help me. Together, we made a good team and got a lot accomplished. Each evening, we would go back to my house. I would transcribe from the notebooks and organize them for later input into the database while Toby entered the water quality data: temperature, dissolved oxygen, and chemicals. He also input the data on the insects found at the stream site.

Insects, like other animals, are classified by their Order, Family, Genus, and then Species; mayflies are in the Order *Ephemeroptera,* (short-lived in Greek); dragonflies, *Odonata*, (referring to their mandibles). When we identified the aquatic insects in the lab we tried to get to the family level, but not everybody was that good at using the key. Students usually only listed the type of insect, by Order, and the quantity found at each site. By the end of the summer we had all of the fifteen years worth of data for Castle Creek completed and input into the database. Not much, but more than what was there before.

And just as Dr. Martha predicted, I began to see a pattern.

"There is always a story," she said. "You just have to look for it."

The stream ecosystem had undergone considerable

change. Early data showed the stream was healthy. It had cool, well-oxygenated waters, holding a diversity of insects that wouldn't tolerate pollution. Until seven years ago, that is, when the abandoned farm fields that bordered the site were converted to an industrial park. The indicators of change were quite obvious; stream temperatures went up as the trees and shrubs that bordered the streambed were cleared, or heavily damaged from construction. When temperatures go up, bacterial decomposition increases, a process that consumes oxygen, so the oxygen levels dropped over time as well. And then deicing salt that ran off the parking lot during spring melt became more apparent as the chloride levels in the stream spiked. The data showed that as a result, the mayfly community diminished over the years until they were nonexistent.

We plodded through the data and spent the night together in my bed. As the summer went lazily by, I started to think more about my future. I had applied to the study abroad program in Australia for the fall semester, and when I got back, I planned to apply to graduate schools for limnology. Toby did not factor into my plans at all. As much as I enjoyed his company, I knew we were not compatible; he and I had very different views on life and how to live it. I was more serious. He was much too playful, joking all the time, and it wore on me. I loved spending time with him but was always left feeling exhausted by the experience, both mentally and physically. I knew it had to end but I was not sure how to break it to him without hurting his feelings.

It was one of the last nights before summer session ended. We all went out to our favorite pizza place to say our good-byes. This was the night I planned to tell Toby that we had to break it off. Afterwards Toby and I took the steep climb down to the campus docks to watch the stars one last time. We were gazing up at the stars, not really talking much when he got on his side and looked at me intensely.

"Emalee, I need to talk to you about something," he said seriously. I turned on my side to look at him. "I want to break up," he said.

"What?" This was supposed to be my line. I wasn't sure if I was relieved or angry. Then I started to laugh.

"Why are you laughing?" he said with hurt in his voice. "I'm sorry if you think this is funny."

"No, no," I sat up and collected my thoughts. "Toby it's ok, really."

"Emalee, you mean a lot to me. It's just that you never seem to be really there for me, you know? You are always so into what you are doing for Dr. Martha's project, and just in general. I don't mean to hurt your feelings or anything, but you can be kinda aloof."

He had read me well. I felt sorry for him then, but deep down we both knew that we were using each other, me for companionship and help with my research, and him for sex. He helped me get over my hurt and despair, the rut I was in all year; he helped me with my project, and I wanted to be kind. So I stole a line from him.

"Toby," I said. "I get it, and I understand. I'll miss you though, you're the best."

I stopped by Dr. Martha's office to say good-bye and tell her about my plans. She was glad that I decided to apply to graduate school and agreed to provide a reference. Because Hobart and William Smith was an undergraduate school, there was no chance for me to continue my research with her there, but she agreed to be my mentor wherever I ended up going to school.

"Please take copies of all the data with you, and I entrust you with the notebooks, but please don't lose anything!" she said. I think at that stage in her life she had no illusions of trying to publish on her own. She had already proven herself to be a great scientist; it was time for her to pass the torch, and if someone like me was willing to take it and run with it all the better for her. At least her relentless data collecting would come to some use.

I had just enough time to go to my home in Rochester and pack before being picked up by a high school friend who was heading to New York for college himself and would drop me at the airport to meet with my classmates and faculty heading to Australia. Laurel tried to talk me into coming to the lake for a few days before I left, but I did not want to go back. I was afraid I would be haunted by memories of Stuart. Audrey came to see me off and help me pack. Surprisingly, Karl came with her. I could not remember a time he had been to our house in Rochester. We spent a few days shopping for things I would need for my fieldwork in Australia. Then we went out to dinner and celebrated my departure. The two of them caught me up on the gossip around the lake.

"Karl, what's happening to the development at the marina? Did the Lowells sell their land to the developer?" I asked. He smiled.

"Well, a group of Amish businessmen have bought the Lowell property and plan to put in vineyards," he said.

"Amish? How did that happen?" I asked. I was surprised by that turn of fortune. I saw a lot of Amish driving around in their buggies, or toiling with horse and plow in their fields, while we were out doing our field-work in the stream sites around Seneca Lake. However, I never thought I would see Amish families settle in Canandaigua.

"Banks love to loan the Amish money because they're a good credit risk. They hate to have debts so they always pay back their loans, and on time. And I know quite a few Amish families near Lancaster County from my real estate dealings there. I happened to read about a group of young Amish men, working at a winery in Lancaster County. They were forced to look for work off their own farms when they started to outgrow the land their family owns. The Amish are eager for new land and business opportunities. There is not enough to pass on to their growing families in Lancaster and the prices are outrageous, much more than here, at least for now," he continued. "So I approached a few of them and made a business deal." He looked at me slyly. I was not sure what all of this meant, but one thing I did know: the marina development was in peril without the Lowell land, and that is what Karl wanted to ensure.

Audrey informed me that Peter was becoming famous. He had sold a few of his paintings and already had a following. "He is also dabbling in interior design, from what his mother tells me," Audrey said. This didn't surprise me; he loved to manipulate space.

She knew nothing of Claire. But I did. Claire had written me several times over the year. At first her letters were cheerful, full of information about Peter and all of his projects, his success and acceptance by the art crowd in New York. But then the letters became increasingly sarcastic, and hinted at a resentment towards Peter and his growing fame. She did not sound happy, but she did not say why. When I called her to ask how her writing was going, she sounded evasive, although she was still in school.

"I'm still writing, but not enjoying it as much as I used to," was all that she said to me on the phone.

"But why?" I asked.

"I don't have any stories I want to write, my life here is too dull," she said. Dull? I thought, how could New York City with Peter be dull? Maybe if she was comparing her career to Peter's it was dull. I told her as much.

"Look, I know what it was like to be Peter's companion, how everyone adores him once they meet him. It's easy to become second fiddle. Even you were under his spell once I introduced the two of you," I reminded her. "But you have to find your own friends, and get your own life, outside of Peter's shadow."

She scoffed at that, "You really are naïve Emalee, aren't you? You don't know what I'm talking about, you don't understand."

I was confused by her defeatist attitude. This was not like the Claire I knew. I missed the old Claire, I missed Peter, and I missed the times we all spent together, Stuart, Peter, Claire and I, boating around the lake, laughing at each other's jokes, caring about each other's ambitions. It seemed like a lifetime ago. I was glad I was leaving for another continent.

CHAPTER TEN

One learns to accept the fact that no permanent return is possible to an old form of relationship; and more deeply still, there is no holding of a relationship to a single form. —Anne Morrow Lindbergh

My senior year flew by. My time in Australia was spent exploring the coral reefs, learning how to identify sea life. But it made me realize that I had no interest in marine biology; I wanted to stick to freshwater. So when I got back for my spring semester, I put all of my efforts into applying to graduate schools that had field stations near lakes. The top two on my list were Cornell, which had a field station on Oneida Lake, and Buffalo State which hosts the Great Lakes Center Field Station on Lake Erie. Lake Erie attracted me because I remembered Dr. Martha telling me that the mayflies had once become extinct there and were now making a comeback. I thought it might be interesting to find out why. I spent my spring semester emailing prospective faculty mentors, and studying for my graduate student entrance tests. In the end, I chose Buff State because they offered me the most attractive financial incentive, a tuition stipend for being a teaching assistant, and research stipends during the spring and summer months. I only had to worry about room and board and I had that covered by my parents' life insurance.

In the midst of my busy final semester I ran into Toby at a local cafe. He came up to me and gave me a big hug. He seemed so happy to see me. I was not sure if I expected less from him or not. Either way, I was glad to see him too. We talked about my plans, he told me about his, when a pretty dark haired freshman came up to him and tugged at his shirt.

"Oh, hey Sarah," he acknowledged her, "Sarah, this is Emalee."

"Hi," I said. She nodded and gave me a wan smile.

"Sarah and I are in the spring production together. You should definitely come see it Emalee," he said.

"Maybe I will," I responded, knowing that I wouldn't and that Sarah did not want me to.

"Well," I said, "it was nice to see you again Toby." I kissed him lightly on the cheek, just out of spite towards Sarah.

He blushed. They left me standing there and headed towards the exit of the cafe. I noticed he had his hand on her ass as they walked out the door.

- *Part Three Erie* -

CHAPTER ELEVEN

In everyone's life at some point, an inner light goes out. It's then burst into flame by an encounter with another human being. We should all be thankful for those people who rekindle the inner spirit. —
Albert Schweitzer

I left my home in Rochester that June in a new car, a Ford Escape, a graduation present from Audrey and Karl, to start a summer session in graduate school at Buffalo State. Audrey had given it to me as a surprise one day, leaving the keys on the counter with a letter she had written:

Dear Emalee,
Out of great sorrow sometimes comes great joy. When I lost my only brother, you also lost your father. But in the midst of this tragedy we had each other. You have been such a blessing to me. I had the honor of watching you mature from a shy teen to a confident young woman. I cannot take any credit for this transformation; yet, I hope that my love for you helped you through these past seven years since your parents' deaths. It wasn't until you left for college that I realized how much you meant to me, your constant presence, your willingness to do

things with me, an old woman, to share my life means more than anything to me. You have become such a beautiful young woman. I know that your father and mother would be so proud of all you have accomplished. I love you very much and will miss you and our time together at the lake.

Love,
Audrey

At the time I read the letter I thought about my mother, how she let go of my hand at Nursery school that day, and how she had missed my graduation. She would have been proud, I thought, that I made it all the way. Until I read this letter I hadn't thought how my absence from the lake was affecting Audrey. I just assumed she was kept busy with Karl.

During my two-hour drive to Buffalo, I had a lot of time to think and I realized how much I missed my summers at the lake, and my time with Audrey. Her hobbies were things that I enjoyed as well. I liked helping her garden, and liked to watch her sail on the lake. I liked to stand by her in the kitchen cooking a meal, and sitting on the screened porch with her while we ate it. She was my only connection to life with my parents, and she quietly filled a void for me, one I hadn't realized was so big until I received her letter. I felt overwhelmed with guilt for not spending more time with her these past couple of years. And in the midst of all of my reflecting, the Dave Matthews Band came on the radio with their song '*The Dreaming Tree*' and in my tortured state of mind, the song reminded me of Stuart. And the sign along the Thruway said '*Welcome to Buffalo, an All America City*' and I wondered what the hell that meant, and why I was heading there?

And I started to cry, and didn't stop until my exit for Buffalo came into view and I had to focus my attention on where I was going before I got lost.

I had a research assistantship set up thanks to Dr. Martha's connections, and was going to live in a dorm suite with three other women students. We shared a common kitchen and living area, and two bathrooms, but separate bedrooms. I shared my bathroom with a woman named Patrice. Patrice was petite, perfectly proportioned, and pretty. She looked like she belonged in a T.V. commercial for Ivory soap. She had a voice that became high pitched when she got excited, which she often did, and it made my skin crawl. But everyone that met her, including me, couldn't help but like her; she was so sweet.

We hit it off right away. She reminded me of Laurel, although Laurel, thank god, did not have that high pitched voice, and did not attract so much attention from men. Patrice on the other hand, always seemed to have a man staring at her wherever we went. She was in graduate school for education. She wanted to be an Elementary teacher. And she was trying to catch up with her studies by staying for summer school. She also had a boyfriend named Tom, who she talked about all the time. He was going to be coming for the second session of summer school. In the meantime, Patrice and I spent a lot of time together.

We explored the city life of Buffalo, and hung out at the local beaches on Lake Erie. The lake was enormous. One of the five Great Lakes, it's a shallow lake that ends at Niagara Falls, emptying into the Niagara River, which then winds its way to Lake Ontario.

Our other two roommates, Julie and Sue, were studying in the psychology department. They would sometimes join us. One night we all went out to eat and we talked about our day. Patrice was working at a day camp in the mornings and taking classes in the afternoon. She spent her mornings manipulating play-doh, making boon-doggle, and catching butterflies with kids. Similarly, my other two roommates, Julie and Sue were working with kids, conducting psychological tests on them. One test they told us about that night was called the 'marshmallow experiment.' Researchers refer to this often as a classic study of children's ability to delay gratification. It was first done on kids in the early 1970s by some psychologists at Stanford University, and has been replicated by numerous researchers ever since.

"We take three and four year olds, place them in a room, and offer them a marshmallow. Then we tell them that if they wait twenty minutes, without eating the marshmallow in front of them, they will get another marshmallow," Sue explained.

"What's the point?" Patrice asked. I thought she should know, considering this was the age group she intended to work with for the rest of her life.

"The point is," continued Julie, butting into Sue's explanation — they had a habit of finishing each other's sentences — "that if they can wait the twenty minutes then they have the aptitude for delaying gratification, a skill they will need throughout their lives."

"How can you say this one experiment proves that they have this ability?" I asked.

"Because research has shown it to be true," Julie said, neglecting to volley the conversation back to Sue. "When they first did this experiment they followed these kids throughout the teen and adult lives and found that the ones that did not eat the marshmallow right away, and waited for the second, were more likely to do well in school, get better grades, and do well in their careers."

"Yes," Sue jumped in while Julie was taking a sip of her beer, "and many of those that couldn't wait for the second marshmallow ended up with unwanted pregnancies, poor grades and had problems the rest of their lives."

That seemed like a pretty severe conclusion to a study

done with marshmallows. And why, if the study had been replicated since the 1970s and ended in a forgone conclusion, would they continue to torture children with this dilemma? I tried to relate it to my own life. What would I have done with the marshmallow? It reminded me of that day back in Nursery school, with my mother holding my hand, and my own impatience with getting on with the day and letting her go. I wondered if this was a sign that I was destined for trouble. I had, after all shown great restraint when it came to Stuart, patiently waiting to tell him how I was feeling, and look how that ended. I had at least avoided the unwanted pregnancy, thanks to Claire's counsel.

"So what do you do all day?" Julie asked. I was getting tired trying to follow the two of them, so it was a respite for me to talk about my own research. As I started to explain a typical day out in the field collecting insects at streams leading into Lake Erie I saw their eyes glaze over and wander, anything but listen to me. My research on insects wasn't as intriguing as children fighting over play-doh, or torturing young minds over marshmallows.

"So let me get this straight," Patrice cut in, "you collect insects from creeks, count how many you have of certain types, and if you have the right types it means the creek is clean?" She summed it up for me, in a way that was both brief and beautifully simple. Sue and Julie looked at her, then at me, Patrice caught us all off-guard; she had actually been listening.

CHAPTER TWELVE

The interpreter must beware lest he read into his subject elements that are more the product of heart than mind. —John A. Weeks

The question came like a torrent, sweeping up a student in the front row.

"Why is it more likely that avian species will practice monogamy than mammals?"

We all waited with bated breath to see if she could answer it. This was the big moment, first thing in the morning when Professor Smith belted out a question from his podium in the front of the lecture hall, looked at his roster and randomly picked a student to answer. If you were present, which you needed to be in order to pass the class in wildlife biology, then you had a one-in-fifty chance of being picked. We all shrank in our seats with discomfort. Some of us knew the answer, of course, because we had done the reading the night before. Others, after finishing their research projects, decided to blow this one off, take a chance they might not get picked, and headed out to a bar. I never took that chance with this class, this Professor. I hated the idea that I might get picked one day. He had a tendency to become sarcastic when a student didn't know the answer, and he scared off a lot of students. By the end of the summer I predicted he was going to lose one-third of the class.

Birds, I discovered the night before while reading the chapter in my textbook on reproductive habits, tend to stay monogamous at least during the breeding season, because they are both involved in the care of their young. In the case of mammals, with the exception of some carnivores, the females will rear the young. They are able to produce milk, and do not need the male to help with feeding. The female student, I could see from my vantage point in the third or fourth row, was blushing, caught off guard. She stumbled a bit with her answer. We all wondered if she had read the textbook and indeed, if she had, did she even comprehend it? The textbook was long, tedious, and technical. We were racing through subjects at lightning speed, trying to cram in, during a three-hour-per-day, five-week session, the life history patterns of wild animals, material that is usually covered over the course of a fifteen-week semester. It was no wonder many students got lost in the lectures and readings and gave up.

Professor Smith heaved a heavy sigh, but before he could make a snarky comment that would have ruined the poor woman's day, a hand went up in the back of the room and someone called his name.

"Professor Smith," a male student from the back waved his hand, "I think I know the correct answer."

The lecture hall echoed with the sound of moving bodies as we all turned in unison to see who was feeling brave that morning. I glanced at a tall, lanky student with sandy brown hair. He looked vaguely familiar to me but I was not sure why. After reciting, practically verbatim, the textbook answer, the class let out a collective sigh of relief. At least that part of the day was over. The rest was spent listening to the professor drone on, from one PowerPoint slide to another, an outline of each chapter we had read the night before.

As far as I could tell, if I could make it past the question and answer period, and regurgitate the lectures on the tests, I had a chance at an A in this class. I was always good at memorizing material, I had a photographic memory, and I could manage to stay awake during lectures. If I found myself wandering off in my head to other thoughts — my parents, Aunt Audrey, my summers at Canandaigua, the cool fresh waters, or Stuart — I spread my hands in an acrobatic exercise, and turned my neck back and forth to bring blood back to my brain. It usually worked. It seemed as if I thought of Stuart at least once a week, if not everyday, even if it was only a fleeting moment. Something, anything, an object, a person's gesture or smile, or a picture, would trigger a memory of him.

After the lecture that day I had field research and then I had allowed myself to be talked into a game of ultimate Frisbee on the quad with Patrice, her boyfriend Tom, and his friends. I had not met Tom yet, but I felt like I already knew him, since that was all that Patrice talked about. She had literally been counting down the days until he showed up for second session. She had a cat calendar, (she loved cats and kittens), and she would pull it off the bulletin board hanging over her bed and mark a big X over the day's date at the end of every evening.

I regretted that I had agreed to play ultimate Frisbee; it was turning out to be a hot summer day and I wanted instead to head a half hour south on the highway to Evangola State Park on Lake Erie and swim. Lake Erie is the fourth largest of the five Great Lakes. It's warmer and shallower than Seneca or Canandaigua, weedier. Sometimes when I went to swim, the water was so green from the algae, it looked like pea soup, but I didn't mind. The weeds were inevitable, due to the warm, shallow waters. The lake's drainage area spans four States and the

Province of Ontario, a huge land area to drain into a lake. As a result, the lake is assaulted by a myriad of pollutants, including runoff from farmland enriched by commercial fertilizers, storm water outfalls that cleanse the city streets of their debris, sewage treatment plants, along with all of the manufacturing industries lining the shorelines in cities like Buffalo, Cleveland, and Toledo. How intriguing, as well as grotesque, that the same bodies of water we drink from are where we dump our waste. The great volume of water in Erie is what keeps the lake in an at least somewhat healthy state.

After a brief dinner at the suite, Patrice was practically dragging me to the quad for the game. She was beside herself with glee and the anticipation of seeing Tom again, which quite frankly, I could not understand, since she had just spent the night before with him at his apartment; showing up at our suite around six AM after what must have been an eventful night.

"Oh my God, wait 'til you meet him," she squealed at me, "you are gonna love him."

She chatted away in what reminded me of the one-way conversations I used to have with Toby. I felt too tired to contribute with the same level of energy. As we approached the quad, a small group of guys playing Frisbee came into view, along with a few female students that I recognized from my wildlife biology class. The brave student from this morning's lecture was playing. He looked better close up. He had an athletic build, tall and muscular, which with his summer tan set him apart from the rest. He looked over at us and waved at Patrice. It was Tom.

The first thing I thought when he came up to greet us and stood by Patrice to shake my hand was: 'My god, it's Ken and Barbie, together on the quad.' His hair was a bit matted and tendrils along the crown of his head and nape of his neck were curling from the sweat, which was oozing out of every pore. They looked made for each other: he, tan, athletic, sandy-haired and handsome, with a broad, white smile: she, perfect, petite, blonde and tan as well. My feelings of inadequacy were compounded by their perfection.

We went out to a bar after the game.

"You were pretty good at that," Tom told me later. Patrice was pouting, she sucked at Ultimate Frisbee, which made me wonder why she wanted so badly to play.

"Thanks, I used to play Frisbee on the lake. We would stand in the lake for hours tossing a Frisbee around."

The whole team sat around the bar drinking pitchers of beer and eating pizza. The men, as usual were swarming around Patrice, who obligingly talked their ears off about some upcoming fundraising event she was organizing for the nursery school on campus. I couldn't help but notice how good she was at seeking attention, while providing it as well, endearing herself to the company around her. In the meantime, Tom and I quietly compared notes on Professor Smith and the wildlife biology class we were taking.

"I can't stand that guy," Tom said, "I had a great professor back at the College of Environmental Science and Forestry in Syracuse. He took much more interest in his students and was doing some great research projects of his own. I would bet that windbag Smith hasn't seen field work since after he published his first paper and got tenure."

"All I know is that I have become addicted to coffee this summer. I drink it while studying at night, and while I'm in class, just to stay awake. So what," I asked him, "made you decide to become a veterinarian?"

"He grew up on a farm." Patrice came up beside him. She must have taken conversational cues from Sue and Julie. He glanced down at Patrice, hanging on to his arm, gave me a look that said, excuse her, and continued.

"We had a crop farm, mostly hay, corn, alfalfa. But my

dad liked to keep animals — goats, chickens, he even raised turkeys at one time. I took care of a lot of them, and enjoyed it. So I think it was my calling."

"You should see his family's farm. It's absolutely amazing. I'm always telling him I want to take my kids on a field trip to his farm. I've never seen tractors so big; I know the boys in my class would love to see it!" The loud bar and the alcohol were causing Patrice's vocal chords to reach a higher octave, if that was even possible. She squeezed his arm.

The combination of the heat at the bar, Patrice's voice, the long day, and the thought of all that reading ahead made me feel tired, so I told them I was heading home.

"We'll walk you back," Tom insisted. Patrice chatted the whole way home about Tom's farm and his plans to be a vet as if she had predestined his life's work.

Tom left us at the door of our suite and brushed a kiss lightly on Patrice's cheek. I could tell she was hoping for more than that. She plopped on the couch and gave out a long sigh. I picked up my textbook.

"You're going to read now?" she asked.

"I have to for this class," I said. I hoped she would go into her room, or find something to do besides bother me. I did not want to go to the library that night to work.

"What did you think of Tom?" She would not leave me alone.

"I like him," I said sincerely. I really did. After spending time with him though, I could not help wondering how these two ended up together. Except for their looks, they were in no way alike. "How did you two meet?"

"We met in college. He was in a fraternity and my sorority did a lot of fundraising with them. We ended up dating, and when he decided to come here for his veterinary degree I applied for my master's in teaching. What about you?"

"What about me?"

"Do you have someone special in your life, a boyfriend perhaps?"

I thought of Toby and Stuart, "No."

"Well I don't understand that. You are so pretty, fun, and nice."

Those were qualities I never associated with myself.

"Thanks Patrice, but I guess no one else sees it that way. Frankly, I am not really looking to date, I'm too busy."

"You know there is this great guy, one of Tom's friends in the Vet school who would be perfect for you. Why don't I set the two of you up on a date?"

"No thanks, Patrice." As much as I appreciated her concern for my love life, I didn't want her to set me up with a complete stranger.

She was not deterred. "I'll talk to Tom about it; I know he would think it was a great idea."

Tom must not have thought it was such a great idea, because the only dates I had for the rest of that summer were with my suite mates. Julie, Sue, and I ended up spending a lot of time together, cooking dinners, going out for a beer, and swimming in the lake whenever we got the chance, while Patrice and Tom spent their waking hours together. There was a two-week break before fall term, and I had to decide what to do: go to the lake or stay put. I hadn't heard much from or about Stuart since the last letter he sent me the year before. But I did keep in touch with Audrey by phone and she supplied me with news.

"The family is staying tight-lipped about the whole drowning affair," she said. "Stuart is doing well in Switzerland and did not come back all summer."

I guessed the memory of his beloved cousin on the bottom of the lake haunted him, especially if it was his unborn child that died along with her.

"Oh, and you would never guess what's happening at the Lowell property. The Amish are already putting in grapevines."

'Yes.' I thought, on the site where Stuart was going to build his house with a view; a place I had day-dreamed we might share together.

"Audrey, I would love to see you, and come to the lake, but it would be best for me to stay on campus to work on my research." As much as I wanted to see Audrey, I knew that I needed to stay focused, and my nostalgia for the lake, the way things were, would only cloud my vision.

Our last night before the break, with no papers, whining kids, or mean professors to contend with the next day, we decided to go out to eat. Patrice was not her usual bubbly self.

"Tom is not coming with me to visit my folks like he said he would," she told us that night. "I'm just not sure where we stand anymore," she sobbed. "I mean, when we came here I thought it would be great, that I would finish my degree and wait for him to finish his and then we would get married. But this summer he has been so distant; it's like he doesn't love me anymore, and I don't know what to do about it."

I found that confession hard to believe. Although Tom never talked to me about Patrice, except the occasional remark about some date they had together, I knew that Patrice was madly in love with him. How could anyone like Tom miss that? He was too perceptive, so why would he be leading her on that way? It seemed insincere on his part, and I didn't think he was an insincere person. It was not his character, but then again, as Claire once told me, what did I know about human behavior?

"Patrice," Sue said, trying to console her, "you know vet school is not the same as getting a masters in education. There are a lot of lab assignments, time spent in clinics. I have a friend in the same program and believe me I never see him."

"I'm trying to be patient, but I think there's something else keeping Tom from me. I'm afraid he is seeing someone else." Patrice was not to be consoled. This bordered on paranoia as far as I was concerned.

"Patrice, Tom doesn't have time to have an affair," I told her. She became extremely drunk, which was not like her, so we half-walked, half carried her home, dragged her into her bed, closed the door, rolled our eyes, and with a sigh of relief that we did not have to listen to her anymore, finished making our plans for the next two weeks.

CHAPTER THIRTEEN

Sometimes you call on those you'd never know to come to you in place of those you've loved. — Daniel Halpern

I had hardly touched the database all summer because of my courses and fieldwork. These two weeks were my chance to catch up. Dr. Martha and I corresponded, and with her help I started writing an outline for a paper to submit to a scientific journal. We would share comments via email: I would send her a draft, she would send back comments and questions that would make me delve deeper into the data. I loved the work, and I loved working with her. She had a knack for asking the right questions, like Audrey did, to make you think for yourself. She never revealed the answers; that would have been too easy.

I was working in the library one morning and decided to take a break. As I was strolling over to the cafeteria I ran into Tom.

"Hey," he said with surprise, "what are you doing here?"

"I could ask the same of you," I said. I had no idea he

was going to be on campus; Patrice never revealed that part during her crying jag the week before.

"I had to stay and catch up on some lab work and volunteer for my internship, it's a lot of work to be in vet school," he said. He looked tired, a bit worn out. I wondered if it was because he missed Patrice.

"Well, it was nice seeing you again," I said. I started to walk towards my destination, and he followed me.

"Where are you going now?" he asked. I told him I was famished.

"Let me come with you, please? I really need a break and someone to talk to besides a dead cat," he laughed. I laughed with him and we went to get some food. I found him easy to talk to, especially with Patrice absent, she always managed to claw her way into any conversation he started.

"I'm so glad that we're done with the Wildlife Biology class," he said.

"I never asked you this, but why didn't you stay at your undergraduate school if you liked it so much?"

"No Vet school."

"How did you meet Patrice then?" She hardly seemed the type to attend a school of forestry; from what I gathered, her idea of the outdoors was a playground.

"Well, I belonged to a fraternity and she belonged to a sorority at Syracuse University and we met at some party." He looked out at the crowds in the café. "I didn't think she would follow me here," he admitted. This was the first time he ever talked to me about her, and his body language told me that it was unsafe to enter this territory. I was sorry I brought it up.

"So what are your plans for the semester?" I asked. He looked back at me and smiled. He had a fabulous smile.

"Well, you won't be seeing much of me I'm afraid. I will be stuck in labs and interning at a local clinic," he said.

"Well then, I'll see you when the semester ends!" I laughed. "But don't make yourself too scarce, Patrice won't like it." As soon as I let that out I regretted it.

He scoffed for a second, thought on it, turned to me, and said, "Hey, what are you doing for dinner tonight?" His question took me aback. Was he asking me out to dinner? He really must be lonely without Patrice. I agreed to meet up with him later.

As it turned out, we spent the next several days having dinner together. We began to seek each other out at lunch in the only open cafeteria at school. We would casually say hi and then, inevitably, we would find a way to meet later. We were both lonely and bored; both of us were working hard, and most of our friends were gone until the fall semester started. We either came to my place or went to his apartment to cook. It was a great chance to unwind after a long day of research. We shared a similar interest in nature, and it was wonderful to have someone to talk to about my research. He would listen and make suggestions about my work. He even offered to read my paper. The two weeks flew by. I had a nagging feeling that maybe I should feel guilty about all of the time he was spending with me instead of Patrice, but our relationship was purely platonic.

It was late September, when a call from Audrey broke my routine.

"A landslide crushed Karl's camp."

"How did that happen?" I asked.

"Oh, landslides happen every once in awhile. They usually don't land on buildings, but we did have a lot of rain these past two weeks," she said.

"We've had a lot of rain before," I said.

"Yes, but this has probably been building over time, and the storm just blew everything out. There are a lot of springs along the cliffs at Karl's camp and they just busted loose from their seam. A huge chunk of the hill came crashing down and landed on his place. The road going in is a mess. I know you are busy, but we could really use your help with the clean-up. Karl only has his motorcycle up here and my car doesn't have four-wheel drive."

That weekend I traveled the two hours down the thruway to Canandaigua, picked them up in my Ford Escape and took them to the scene of the disaster. There was not much to salvage.

The first clue that things were not good was the road leading to the camp. It was a seasonal road made of dirt and crushed stone. The culverts couldn't handle the volume of water coming down from the hills, so parts of the road had washed away during a torrential downpour, the final assault after two weeks of rain.

"Let me get out here and lead you down the road. There may be sections that are washed away," Karl said. He got out of the car, put his hand on the roof as he managed his way towards the front; it was painful to watch him with his bad leg, limping ahead of us to look for signs of wash-outs. The road was slow-going; we could see the aftermath of the torrential rains all around us. His place was at the vortex of the storm's wrath.

"A river of mud," as one neighbor put it, "came sweeping down the hill," and as water will, took the path of least resistance – the road provided a straight shot to Karl's camp at the end. The springs from the hillsides behind his camp became torrents that uprooted large trees. When we finally approached his place we could see that a large oak had landed on the roof of his kitchen. There were boulders, stones, shale, and debris in the kitchen. The deck, which had broken off its joints from the deluge of water, was twenty feet down the cliff. Any day now another jolt of rain would probably send it hurling into the water below. Living at the southern end meant great views, and some risks, but I don't think anyone, including Karl, had expected this to happen.

We picked our way through the kitchen, however it was treacherous to venture much further into the shell of his camp.

"I don't think I have ever seen such destruction before," Karl said despondently.

"Will your insurance cover any of this?" I asked.

"No, 'fraid not. Looks like all is a total loss, folks." He could not rebuild.

As Audrey and Karl looked around for anything to salvage I wandered to a clearing in the debris and looked down the lake at the mouth of the West River. The lake was calm, the water like glass. It was hard to think that a place of such peaceful splendor could herald such destruction. There were a couple of canoeists gliding along the water. I felt a twinge of remorse for things long gone, thinking about the canoe trip with Stuart, our joy at seeing the views from this end of the lake. I could understand why Karl would want to live here.

Back at Audrey's camp Karl did not say much.

"Karl, you know you can stay here with me, we will figure this all out together," Audrey assured him. I had nothing to offer but my condolences. Feeling completely useless, I left them in the kitchen talking over their next steps, and headed back to school.

I got back to campus and right into my routine again, classes, labs, papers. Fall semester was busy for all of us, including Patrice, which was a good thing because it took her mind off Tom, who was ever absent from our suite, unlike during the summer when he would stop by once or twice a week to pick up Patrice for a night out. I had not run into him anywhere since the end of summer session so it was a pleasant surprise when I opened our suite door and he was there. He looked handsome standing in the doorway, dressed in a collared golf shirt and khakis. Patrice had not told me he was coming, but they must have made plans to go somewhere.

"Come on in," I said delighted to see him. "Where have you been all semester? We've all missed you here."

Sue and Julie were in the kitchen making dinner, "Tom!" they said in unison. He seemed glad to see us as well. He looked like he had lost some weight. At this point in the semester, the crush of the workload must have been heavy. I knew that I was bogged down in lab assignments and studying for mid-terms.

"Hey guys," he said, "I have missed you all too. I've been holed up in labs, couldn't wait to get out tonight."

"Where are you going with Patrice?" Sue came out of the kitchen to ask him. She sat down with a bowl of ice cream. I wondered what happened to the dinner she was supposed to be making. Just then Patrice came waltzing into the living room. She looked stunning. She was wearing a short, tight, black dress that barely covered her derriere. She must have been saving this little number for a special occasion. I had never seen her wear it before. Tom obviously hadn't either: his eyes popped out of his head when she walked in.

"Well, you look great!"

Patrice beamed, "Thank you." By then Julie had entered the living room and was also gawking at Patrice.

"It's our second year anniversary," Patrice said, looking over at us as we stood speechless. Sue, Julie and I looked on in envy as Tom took her arm and escorted her through the door.

There is a saying that only in Upstate New York can one experience all four seasons in a week. Such was the case the week before finals that spring semester. It even had the audacity to snow on Mother's Day. The second week of May started off cheery enough: the temperature was in the mid-70s and the sky was as blue as the Caribbean sea. For two days it stayed this way — no clouds in the sky — enticing the students to break out their shorts and t-shirts and prance around campus. We fooled ourselves into thinking summer was coming; or was here already. By the third day the temperatures had dropped twenty degrees, a prologue for what was to come. The air was crisp and cold, like fall. Then on the fourth day the weatherman turned on us, the clouds moved in and cast a pall on the once sunny quad, and the students' mood. The air became cold and clammy, the worst combination, and one that Buffalo has down to a science. Finally the clouds let go of their precipitation, and it rained for two days, the temperatures dropping into the 40s. Typical spring weather for Buffalo. And then it happened, the locals said they had never seen it before, snow on Mother's Day — two inches worth. It melted the next day but psychologically stayed with us.

It was a shame because what the campus community really needed was sunshine. The winter had been brutal that year. When the cold air came sweeping down from Canada in December, the tremendous heat Lake Erie stored all fall created a recipe for lake effect snowstorms. The cold, dry air soaked up the lake's warm waters and dumped it as snow on the nearest landmass — Buffalo. We were inundated and it did not stop until March.

In the beginning, students took to the snow like fish to water. Buffalonians, even transplants like me, are a hardy bunch, and there was no denying that on sunny, clear, cold days, the snow looked like a blanket of white glitter. On days like these, the undergrads would steal a lunch tray from the cafeteria to use as a sled. And although the terrain in Buffalo is relatively flat, they would manage to find snow packed knolls on campus to fly down.

But by late February the students had had enough of the winter wonderland and were starting to jump out of their skins. Julie, Sue, Patrice and I were starting to feel it as well: cabin fever. Sue and Julie — who did all of the cooking — started to argue over ingredients. Patrice, ever the cheerleader (she was going to make a great kindergarten teacher one day), tried to cheer us up with games of Scrabble and Euchre. But she began to wear thin as well, her moods dictated by the appearance, or lack thereof, of Tom.

We occasionally saw him at the local bars, including one of our favorite haunts, Mr. Goodbar. Patrice would make a plan to meet him and invite us along, we would do anything to get out of the suite. The bars in Buffalo are like pressure valves for the City — a place for people to meet, feel somewhat human in all that endless lake effect, and let off some steam.

One cold night in March we all met at Mr. Goodbar and drank way too much beer. We danced until two AM and called a taxi. When we reached campus Patrice told the driver to let Sue, Julie and me out while she stayed on with Tom.

Tom immediately objected, "Patrice, I have way too much work tomorrow." Tom was obviously pulling away, and she hated it. She dejectedly left the cab and came home with us.

Even though it snowed on Mother's Day, summer was inevitable, and I had to make some decisions about what I would do. I planned to stay on campus again, work on my paper for publication, and continue my research and coursework. Karl was now living with Audrey and I felt that they could use the privacy. After all, I had disrupted their plans when I came into their life unexpectedly at the age of fifteen. I felt this was their chance to make up for lost time. While breezing down the halls of the science wing after meeting with my faculty advisor, I happened upon a notice hanging on the bulletin board asking for volunteers. It read: 'Volunteers Wanted to Assist in Wildlife Research Project, Algonquin Provincial Park, May 20-June 1st.' There were hanging tabs with a number to call and the initials T.W. and not much else to go by. It had been a long, cold spring and a change of scenery might be good for me. I hesitated in front of the sign, pulled off one of the tabs, and put it in my wallet. A week went by and I had not thought about the notice to volunteer until the tab with the number fell out of my wallet one morning while I was getting coffee. 'Why not?' I thought, my research could wait two weeks, and I needed to rejuvenate a bit after finals. I had never visited Algonquin, never even heard of it before, so what did I have to lose? I pulled out my cell phone and called the number, waiting for T.W., whoever that was, to answer.

"Hello," the man on the other end said. His voice sounded familiar.

"Hello, I'm calling about the sign? You were looking for volunteers for a wildlife research project?" There was a pause of recognition on the other end.

"Oh, yes, yes, I forgot I put that sign up about two weeks ago and have only had a couple of calls. Yes, we're looking for a few volunteers, are you interested?"

"Yes, I think so, can you tell me more about it?" For a brief moment I had a vision of a serial killer luring me to a dark spot on campus only to abduct, rape and stab me to death. I shuddered at the thought. What was wrong with me?

I was about to hang up when the voice on the other end said, "Is this Emalee?"

It was Tom, Patrice's Tom. His last name was never impressed upon me. Williams, yes, that was it, Tom Williams. It took a minute to register, but yes, it was Patrice's Tom on the other end of the line, how did I not recognize his voice, his number?

"Yeah, is this Tom?"

"Yes. A good friend of mine, a professor from my undergraduate school, is looking for volunteers to help him this spring," he continued.

"Really? Well, I'm busy doing my own research, I doubt I'd have time to volunteer," I said trying to erase this call, this conversation. There was no way I was going on a volunteer expedition with Tom, especially with

Patrice tagging along, which was inevitable given her propensity to insert herself in anything he did.

"Then why did you call?" He had a point.

I blew air out of my lungs, not realizing I was holding it in, "OK, I'll bite, what is his research on?"

"Moose."

- Part Four Algonquin -

CHAPTER FOURTEEN

The moose will perhaps one day become extinct; but how naturally then, when it exists only as a fossil relic, and unseen as that, may the poet or sculptor invent a fabulous animal with similar branching and leafy horns, — a sort of fucus or lichen in bone, — to be the inhabitant of such a forest as this! — Henry David Thoreau

A far cry from mayflies, moose may live up to fifteen years and can weigh up to 800 pounds. By 1961 they were extirpated from the Adirondacks in New York due to habitat loss and over-hunting. Jim O'Connell, Tom's mentor and professor of wildlife biology at the College of Environmental Science and Forestry in Syracuse, had made it his passion to follow these magnificent creatures in a remote, Canadian, provincial forest studying their life history and population carrying capacity. At some point, even in the human race, species reach a point where limited resources, disease, and other natural phenomena will place constraints on population growth.

"The last time O'Connell conducted research for his dissertation," Tom explained, "the moose of Algonquin had reached their carrying capacity. Now, a decade later, he has a grant to go back and see what had happened since. He needs volunteers for about two weeks to help him capture and tag the moose. You have to be willing to endure the black flies and mosquitoes though; this is the worst time of year to visit."

I wondered if Tom had asked Patrice to come. It did not take long to find out.

When I broached the subject of her plans after the spring semester ended, she was livid, explaining how "Tom was going off on some moose tracking expedition in the middle of the wilderness, and had not invited her along." Not only had he not invited her, I found out, when she inquired about going, he told her no.

"But I hear he has invited you," she said accusingly.

I tried to calm her down, "Patrice, I had no idea it was Tom organizing this trip when I called to volunteer, I was just responding to a flyer someone put up on the bulletin board in the science wing. There are a number of us going."

This was only partially true. There were only four of us going from campus. I had agreed to drive since I had the newest car. The other volunteers were all meeting us at the site, some of them from Buff State, some from the College of Forestry.

"Besides, field work is what I do. I spend time in the outdoors for my research. It's a far cry from what you do."

She glared at me then. "You don't go around tracking moose, you're doing this to be with him."

Was she serious? I thought.

"I see the way you look at him; you're attracted to him. I can tell." She flailed onto her bed.

There was not much for me to say to this, it was ludicrous. To begin with, except for the brief time we spent last summer, I hardly saw Tom unless he was with Patrice, and I had no time for a relationship, nor did I have any interest. Deep inside I think I was still holding on to hope that Stuart would come back, we would meet in Canandaigua, and spend the rest of our lives together. A hopeless dream, I knew, considering we did not communicate anymore, but one that lingered.

She got over her jealousy by the time we left, wishing us both good-bye as we climbed into my Ford Escape for the long drive to Algonquin. It took us five hours to get there. The other two students were a couple, Connor and Lisa. Birding was Lisa's hobby. She had interned for two summers at the Cornell Lab of Ornithology at Sap Sucker Woods, but she was pre-med. Connor was studying to become an ichthyologist. We taught each other something about our fields. I worked around a lot of fishery students at the Great Lakes Center station so I knew enough about Connor's work. He and his colleagues took canoes with outboard motors and trolled the tributaries with their shocking tools, long poles with electrified metal hoops on their ends. These hoops give off about 150-volts of electric current and the fish are paralyzed for a few minutes, which allows the crew to collect the unlucky fellows in their nets to be tagged, weighed, sexed, and sized. After this nightmare, the fish are released back to the stream. I was not sure which method of collecting aquatic specimens was more inhumane, mine, where we stirred up the streambed to dislodge the unsuspecting insects, i.d. and preserve them in vials on shelves, or his, where the stunned fish are abducted by what to them must seem like alien life forms, then released back to their natural habitat without any understanding of what happened to them while they were out cold.

I also learned a lot about Tom while we were driving. He was very ambitious, serious about his plans to become a vet. It was something he had dreamed about doing since he was young. He also had a sense of humor, telling us all kinds of funny stories about his lab partners and their aversion to the carcasses they had to dissect.

"How can a person go into that field unless they can

handle dissection?" I asked.

He shrugged. "They won't, make it that is."

I shared my work with them, although Tom knew what I did for my research.

"I am glad for this break because I feel like I'm getting a bit bored with the same field research. I spent all spring on the tributaries that lead to the Niagara River. I found some interesting creatures, let me tell you, ones that I never saw before. But my real interest is in the mayflies. They're returning to the tributaries and shoreline of Lake Erie after years of absence."

"What caused their decline?" Lisa asked.

"There are theories. Erie became putrid from all the untreated sewage that the cities had been dumping since industrialization. The sewage caused the lake to turn a bright green by feeding the algae and plant life the nutrients they need to grow. The problem is that when the plants die, they sink to the bottom and decompose, a process that uses up oxygen. At one time, there were 'dead zones' in the lake, places completely devoid of oxygen and the mayflies are sensitive to that. They need well-oxygenated waters to survive. But that stopped, technologies caught up, and the Lake is getting much cleaner. The mayfly is making a comeback." I smiled.

Like the mayfly on Lake Erie, by the turn of the 21st century, moose were repopulating the Adirondacks in New York. Their numbers climbed from fifty to over two hundred in just a decade. This remarkable feat was why O'Connell wanted to revisit his subjects in Algonquin. Since the time of his dissertation, the return of the moose to New York State also meant pressure from hunters to allow a hunting season on the animals. Debates were raging between hunters and preservationists about the ability of the moose to survive this human-induced population control. The moose population in Algonquin was unique in that it was not exploited, due to Provincial law and inaccessibility. Only natives were allowed to hunt, and that was limited. His research on an unexploited population of moose provided a glimpse into the natural factors that contribute to the species' carrying capacity, such as predation by bear or wolves and disease.

Algonquin was a place for loners. The people who lived and worked in and along its borders came for one reason: to be alone in the woods. The only way to get into the interior of Algonquin is by canoe or hiking. There is only one road, running through the southern portion of the park. O'Connell's team of researchers were allowed a small outboard motor boat to conduct their study, but other than that, there were no motorboats allowed.

When we finally reached the outskirts of the Park, we stopped at the Algonquin Outfitters to pick up some gear. Tom knew the place, from his previous field-work with O'Connell.

"Nothing about this place has changed," he said, looking around as we entered.

People dressed in hiking pants and t-shirts, wearing Teva water shoes the likes of which I had never seen before, were milling around the store, some of them looking to purchase hand crafted 'Swift' Algonquin Canoes, a canoe specially designed for this region, to take into the interior. Others were reserving the water taxi to take a group with several canoes to the farthest outpost in the interior for canoe camping.

Tom had told us what to bring, a sleeping bag, change of clothes, shoes that could get wet, rain gear, and wool, not cotton, to repel the moisture that permeated the atmosphere here. But these outdoor enthusiasts took their sport seriously. I saw people stocking up on all kinds of supplies, that Tom had not mentioned we needed: water proof packs, dried food of all kinds, matches, small saws, biodegradable soap, waterproof maps of the park, water filters — it was endless — what was needed for a trip into the wilderness.

A young couple sidled up next to me to look at the water filters on the shelf. I watched them out of the corner of my eye as they quietly talked about the one they had that busted, and how much to spend on a new one. They looked like they had not seen civilization in a while. I was surprised, given the chill in the air — it was after all only the third week of May and we were in Canada — that they were only wearing tattered shorts and Teva sandals. She had on a heavy Aran sweater, the type that was once a creamy white but now looked a dull brownish-grey from the dirt that had accumulated in its fuzz. He was wearing a worn-out sweatshirt with 'McGill University' emblazoned on the front. Their feet were tarnished black from walking in the tannin soaked soils, their calves slim and sinewy from walking in the woods. They must be making a quick trip for supplies after months, if not years, away from the nearest shower, I thought. They both wore their golden-colored hair in dreadlocks, probably easier to handle when you don't own a hair-brush. Their skin was a burnt umber, a color only achieved on fair-skinned people after days without sunscreen. Melanoma waiting to happen. This skin tone served to accentuate their vivid blue eyes. In a moment of motherly instinct, I reached for the sunblock, and was about to say "Here, protect yourself," but they moved to the next aisle.

I couldn't help following them, furtively keeping one eye on their movements as if they were movie stars. I was transfixed by their slight gestures, their inconspicuous purposeful presence. Who were these people? They looked like fraternal twins. Where did they belong? What did their mother think? Are they missed by someone, anyone? What, I allowed myself to day-dream, would happen if I ran away to the woods and never communicated with Audrey, would she worry about me being eaten by a bear? I imagined them running away from some deep, dark secrets, trying to find themselves in the woods. I naively wanted to talk to them about the black flies, mosquitoes and other stinging insects because they seemed fixated on the water filters but I noticed that their legs were swollen from bites. Maybe, they should be investing in bug repellent along with the sunscreen.

My head was spinning from all of the gear, and the fact that I, along with this hapless couple, did not seem to own any of it besides the bare essentials, when Tom reached for my elbow, said, "Let's go," guiding me towards the counter. He had picked up a number of items that I was so worried we needed — for the both of us.

While standing next to Tom at the counter, I was browsing through the display of postcards and came upon a beautiful representation of the Northern Lights bursting over a small mountain terrain with what looked like a wetland covered in snow in the foreground. The hues of green and purple in a backdrop of scarlet blue sky speckled by stars sent me back to the night on Canandaigua Lake. The clerk saw me admiring the cards and said, "You like those?"

"Yes, they're beautiful," I said.

"Well the postcards are reproductions of art work done by Tom Thomson," she nodded in the direction of the walls, which were covered in posters, larger versions of the postcards.

"Thomson lived in these woods about one hundred years ago. That postcard in your hand, called Northern Lights, he painted in 1916 on a cold winter night while camping," she explained.

I picked out Thomson's rendition of the light show from heaven to keep for myself, and other postcards to send to friends and Audrey. With a quick afterthought, I grabbed one more Northern Lights postcard to send to Stuart.

As we were leaving the store we ran into Tom's colleague and mentor, Jim O'Connell. Jim was a compact male. He was average height, sturdy, and from the looks of it, strong. His eyes twinkled when he greeted us. I liked him immediately.

"Well if it isn't Tom. So good to see you made it! I was wondering when you would get here. I am glad we ran into each other, cell phone coverage is spotty up here." He greeted Tom warmly, giving him a handshake and slap on the back.

"I think I would remember how to get to the camp either way Jim. It's only been a year and not much changes around here."

O'Connell turned to me, "And you are?"

"This is Emalee. I told you I was bringing along a few fellow students, hope you don't mind the additional help."

"Of course not," O'Connell seemed pleased as punch that we were there. I imagined he did not get a lot of visitors while he was doing his research, except for these two weeks in late May when he captured and tagged the Moose cows and their calves. Other fellow volunteers started to straggle out of the store. We were introduced to another couple, Dan and Amy from Syracuse; Liz, a colleague of O'Connell's who was on leave from her own research project studying lemurs in Madagascar; and a woman named Bridget, who looked slightly pregnant, but no one dared ask during our greetings: instead we all unconsciously glanced down at her belly. Connor and Lisa came out of the store, we exchanged more greetings and then gathered our contingent together to head to the Algonquin Wildlife Research Station, our base camp on Lake Sasajewun, owned by the University of Guelph.

We followed O'Connell's Ford pick-up back to the base. Along the way we saw the young homeless couple from the store holding their thumbs out for a ride. O'Connell swung over to the side of the road and they jumped into the truck bed and wedged themselves amongst the gear. Tom was driving at this point and the two of us were staring right into their vivid blue eyes.

"Who are all of those people in that store?" Lisa asked. "Why are they all here, in the middle of nowhere during black fly season?"

"Well they are all mostly tourists. A lot of people are here to see the moose. This is the time of year when they come out of the woods to eat the left over deicing salt that has accumulated along Route 60. Some of the people that come here live in the woods year-round, or most of the year, as long as they can survive it. That couple for instance," Tom nodded his head towards the couple in O'Connell's truck in front of us, "probably have been here through the winter and are starting to run out of supplies. You find all kinds of people up here. They spend their lives in the woods, only coming out when they need to go back home and make some money. Or they may be homeless and they find odd jobs to buy more supplies and head back into the woods. You can get lost pretty easily in this wilderness."

I peeled my eyes away from the young couple to look out at the scenery. The forest canopy was different from the Finger Lakes region. It was dominated by coniferous trees; a signature of colder climates and soils that are frozen most of the year. I could distinguish some of the trees thanks to a dendrology class I took in the fall. I always envied people who could identify trees without looking at a field guide, and after one class I realized there are a number of trees distinguishable by their silhouettes, leaves, needles and bark. From my viewpoint I could see pines, both Jack and White, some spruce and fir. Sprinkled in their midst were aspen trees, the leaves trembling in the breeze.

As we passed many small lakes and streams, my mind wandered to Canandaigua. Maybe this was what the Finger Lakes looked like when the first settlers came to the region, a vast expanse of woods dotted with a few Native American settlements, unscathed by human exploitation. I kept looking around for signs of development, maybe a Walmart or Starbucks to remind me that we were in the 21st century. But there was nothing like that here.

The tourist attraction was evident along Highway 60. Dominating the shoulder of the road were moose, some cows with their calves, licking salt that had accumulated along the ditches. They nonchalantly bent down to lick at the salt pools in the ditches, glancing up once in awhile to pay recognition to the cameras the tourists aimed at their faces. Everywhere we looked people were stopping, parking their cars to get out and take pictures.

"Idiots," Tom exclaimed. "They have no idea if that cow will charge or not."

"What do you mean?" Connor asked.

"The only defense for a moose, if it feels threatened, is to charge its target. Their sheer size, strong and powerful legs, which they use to defend themselves, can kill a small bear, even a human, in a matter of minutes." Tom passed the gawkers, refusing to stop himself for our viewing pleasure, and proceeded to the camp, while Connor, Lisa and I plastered our faces to the windows watching in awe as these huge animals idly stood by on the shoulder of the road as if the tourists were nothing but a small nuisance, like gnats.

Every once in awhile we would pass a trailhead sign along the road, and the couple in O'Connell's truck thumped their fists on the cab to signal O'Connell which one of these was their stop. He stopped his truck on the shoulder of the road. They waved at O'Connell, and disembarked from the truck bed, pulling their packs, filled with new supplies, onto their backs. Tom slowed down to wait for O'Connell. The whole time we had been watching the nomads in the back of the truck with quiet curiosity. Our gaze followed them as if they were moose on the side of the road licking salt. They wandered into the forest, the trees swallowing them from our view.

"I have always wondered what it would be like to run away like that," Tom remarked.

Their departure, and our fascination with them reminded me of an Emily Dickinson poem I had to memorize in High School:

The soul selects her own society -
Then - shuts the door -
On her divine majority -
Present no more -

We finally arrived at the base camp. After unpacking our gear, I meandered to a lounge chair on the deck and sat down to catch the end of the day. I turned my face towards the sun and let the rays soak in. Tom followed me out with two beers in his hand. He threw one at me, but missed his mark. It rolled along the floor toward my feet. I picked it up and started tapping the top of the aluminum can 'tap, tap, tap' with my fingertips.

"Do you really think that makes a difference?" he asked me.

"I don't know," I shrugged, "I've just always done it to settle the beer. Let's experiment." I turned the opening of the can away from my face, popped open the lid, and a geyser of beer spurted out.

"Ha!" he said. "Another myth busted." We both laughed as I put my mouth over the opening of the can to catch the foaming beer before it was half emptied.

"It's nice to see you laugh," he said as he dropped himself into the chair next to mine. I stayed silent, looking out at the woods, drinking my beer. "You don't smile much. I've wanted to ask this for a long time: why are you always so sad Emalee?"

No one had ever asked me that before. My close friends already knew why and if they didn't, well Laurel wouldn't dare spoil our fun by asking such things, Peter assumed I didn't care, Claire had other things on her mind, and Stuart, I assumed, didn't want to invade my privacy. I looked over at Tom. He was waiting for an answer. And then, I told him my story, unhurriedly. Telling it felt like the twisting the lid off a bottle of a carbonated beverage, opening it bit by bit, to release the air slowly. It felt good to exhale.

When I finished with the sordid tale of my mother's death, my father's suicide, he looked away, embarrassed that he had asked and said quietly, "I'm sorry."

What more could he say? My confession was a conversation stopper, but O'Connell saved the moment when he flew onto the deck, his arms loaded down with gear.

"There you guys are. I need you to help me get this gear ready for tomorrow." We gladly obliged.

He had a dozen or so collars that would fit a very large dog. They were fitted with mortality-sensing radio devices that would allow him to track death rates of the newborn moose. These were for the calves he planned to tag in the coming weeks. We had to make sure the break-away was working on the collars so that the calves would not choke once they outgrew them. I started to get excited about our adventure in the woods of Algonquin.

CHAPTER FIFTEEN

...the best I can do does not do the place much justice in the way of beauty...— Tom Thomson

Writing postcards is the most unjust form of communication. I stared at the small blank space that only allowed two to three lines at the most once the address was affixed. I had no trouble writing most of the cards, "Hey, hope all is well. I'm deep in the woods chasing moose, see you whenever." But I had not talked to Stuart since my undergraduate days and no matter what I wrote now, there was so much left to say.

Stuart, I wrote (there was no room for salutations),

I am deep in the woods in Canada helping a scientist with his research on moose. Can't begin to describe how beautiful it is here. Saw this and thought about our night on the lake watching the Northern Lights. I miss you. I miss talking with you. I hope you are doing well. Love, Emalee.

I had a dissertation of all of the things I really wanted to say to him: "I wish you could be here to share this with me. I know you would love it here. So your family property was sold; are you sad that you will never get to build your dream house now? What happened to Danielle that night after I left you? Was she carrying your child? Is that why she was so upset that morning? Do you love me as much as I think I love you?"

His lengthy address was in the small address book that I brought in case I needed to call or felt the urge to send letters home. It took up a quarter of the card. The cards were stacked and ready to go in the mail-box at the base camp but sending Stuart's card was going to cost more than a few stamps. The outpost store had a post office and would deliver it, so I tucked it away in my pack until we went back for supplies. I knew Audrey would love to hear what I was doing and I felt bad I could not tell her more than the postcard allowed. She and Karl were now living together at the lake for the summer. She called me before I left to tell me how happy they were. Karl had some ideas on fixing the place up and adding on to the porch. They had their projects and the time to work on them together. They did not need me around.

In the morning, the smell of coffee permeated the camp. I woke up to it, inhaling deeply, my favorite smell. The dawn was just breaking outside my window and although the window was closed, all night I felt the damp chill of the woods surrounding the camp. I grabbed my toothbrush, walked the hall to the bathroom and threw some water on my face to wake up. When I got to the kitchen, Trevor Fields, the overseer of the research station, was stirring a batch of eggs. He grunted, and pointed to the coffee mugs. He clearly was not one for early morning chit-chat, so I took a mug from the shelf, filled it to the brim and went out on the deck. The air was alive with fog, the tree limbs giving the illusion of lifting it up into their canopy.

At the end of the deck, Lisa was placing sunflower seeds in a row on the deck rail. I was about to ask her what she was doing when a small, gray-feathered bird with a white breast and black head came sailing down from a fir tree, and, with great ease, picked up the seed in its beak and flew back to the fir. Each time the bird took a seed, Lisa replaced it with another, leading the bird towards me to see the show. I watched the small bird fly back to its perch in the tree. He swallowed every other seed, the rest he lodged in crevices of the bark that only he seemed to see or know existed. I watched in awe for about ten minutes, before Lisa saw me out of the corner of her eye. She looked over and waved. I did not want to disturb the feeding so I wiped off the dew on one of the deck chairs with the end of my sweatshirt sleeve, and sat down.

When she was all out of seed, she came over to me.

"What are those birds, and why are they so tame?" I asked.

"Those are called Gray Jays. They're indigenous to this forest and one of the few birds that don't migrate south."

"They don't fly south?"

"No, you just witnessed this little one storing some supplies for next winter."

"Really, and how do they find the seeds after so many months?"

"Well, not exactly sure, but the current theory is that they have a special saliva that coats the seeds when they deposit them and this helps them identify their food later on."

A few hours later, Trevor Fields dropped us off in his motorboat on one of the many islands that dotted the landscape. We waited on a trail leading to the woods for radio instructions from O'Connell who was on a small outboard circling the island.

Having a birder in the woods made the experience more enriching. Lisa's knowledge of birds went beyond a study of their habits. At this time of the morning, there was a conversation going on in the trees that only she could interpret. The birds were calling to each other — and Lisa recognized their songs.

"I spent two years with the audio engineer at the Ornithology lab, making recordings of bird calls. You get good at it."

We were treated to the sight of a brilliant blue bird — an Indigo Bunting flitting from one tree to another on the woods' edge. It gave off a whistle, answered by his mate from some other location. Lisa motioned for us to be quiet while she raised her hand in the air and pointed out the high pitched call of the Wood Thrush, a long 'eeee-olay' followed by a trill. Above it all was the chatter of the Gray Jays, calling one another as if in greeting to say 'Hey you're back, now let's get together.' Actually, that is what the birds were doing, Lisa explained.

"They're looking for their mates and the best way to do it in these deep woods is to use a call, for some it's breeding time, for others like the Gray Jay, that have already nested, it's about protecting territory."

"So why did you give up ornithology?" I asked her.

"I decided on med school. Birding won't pay my student loans back."

Liz, the lemur expert, gave a short laugh in agreement. I wondered if she knew something I didn't — was there money in studying lemurs? For that matter was there money in chasing aquatic insects or fish, or moose? I never worried about it because my college was paid for by a life insurance policy. Connor gave Lisa a slight slap on the back.

"That's why I am marrying you," he said, "so you can help pay off mine as well." We all grinned. I heard a strange sound like a creaking door growing louder as it moved towards us.

"What's that bird?"

"That," Tom came close to me and leaned in, "is the

most exotic animal found in this wilderness."

I looked up at him, wondering what strange thing was about to jump out at us.

"A squirrel." He laughed. I gave him a punch in the arm for trying to be smart with me. The radios crackled.

"Tom, you there?" It was O'Connell. He had positioned his boat for the capture and tag operation.

"Here."

"Let's do it then, let me know when you're in position."

Tom knew what we had to do next. He gave us instructions: we were to fan out, one person approximately every ten yards, until we had the width of the island covered. We were to move along at the clip of Tom's lanky paces — ten every thirty seconds, then stop, call each other on the radio and make sure we were still in a line.

"The mother was radio collared last spring with a global positioning unit so we know she is here, presumably with a calf. The idea is to flush them out and force them to the edge of the island. Jim will be offshore waiting to see if they retreat to the water. If so, he will chase them both back, but he may try to capture the calf by boat. We need to keep the mother and calf separated so he can do his work."

It sounded a bit complicated to me. This was nothing like kicking up pebbles in a creek bed to flush out the insects.

"Now, this is important," Tom continued. "If the cow feels threatened, she will charge. If that happens, you need to run fast and stand behind the nearest tree."

I looked over at Bridget, who had finally admitted to us all the night before that she was pregnant. Did she know what she was getting herself into when she signed up?

We entered the woods. It was a bright sunny morning, the birds and the insects were all astir. I had a hat on but it was no protection against the biting black flies. These little monsters may have been seeking their revenge on me, as I had kicked up enough of them in the creeks and streams along Lakes Seneca and Erie. Ironically, they, like the mayflies, prefer cool, well-oxygenated waters and do well in woods like these where there is little human pollution. While conducting my field-work I would see them in their larval stage, attached to rocks in the swift flowing segments of streams. They look like small black strings under water. When they hatch, only the females bite, with a razor-like incision. They need a blood meal before they can lay eggs. At home the flies would occasionally bite me, but this assault was different. We were probably the easiest prey as there are not many other animals to choose from in the deep woods, beside the moose and birds.

I waved one away as I followed Tom; we were in a line now and working our way to the other end of the island. Tom had a small hatchet and was bushwacking a path for us. We used large sticks to push the hanging vegetation, prickly bushes and tree branches out of our way. On the other side of me was Bridget, and next to her Dan and Amy, Connor and Lisa and at the tail end, Liz. Every once in awhile Tom would stop us and tell someone to stay put while the rest of us went ahead. He did this in intervals until I was the last to stay. He left me and walked another ten yards away. We had the width of the island covered. Poor Liz had to wait the longest for us all to get into position. I could only imagine the bug bites she was enduring. Maybe they were nothing compared to what she was used to in the jungles of Madagascar, but they were bad. My new hiking boots were starting to feel damp from the dew that was plastered on the vegetation underfoot. So much for the water resistant spray I had slathered on them the night before. A black fly was following my every move, buzzing and biting my ears. I wished I had a net to cover my face.

Once in position we radioed each other and Tom issued the command for us to move. Every ten paces, we stopped, checked our location in line with the people next to us and kept going this way until we heard a rustle in the brush.

"That's her," Tom whispered over the radios. We all stood still, I could feel my heart pounding. I looked over at Bridget to see how she was holding up. She was shooing at some flies, and waved my way to show she was all right.

"OK, keep moving," he instructed.

By the time we reached the water's edge, the cow was in a panic over her calf. She had led him into the water where O'Connell was making whooping sounds to try to separate them. Trevor was maneuvering his boat to push her away from her calf and back to land. The idea of a panic-stricken, half-ton mother moose back on the island with us did not appeal to me in the least. But Tom seemed to know what he was doing.

"Keep her distracted!" He shouted at us as O'Connell lifted the calf into his boat. I felt sorry for the cow moose, turning her great body this way and that, not sure what to do, the target of her fear being the man in the boat on the water with her calf half-pulled into it. We managed to circle the animal, waving our hands in the air. We kept her from running back into the water to protect her calf. She made a pathetic sound, like a milk cow, injured and dying in a farm field might make. O'Connell quickly collared the frightened calf, and used what looked like a hole punch to affix an ear-tag identifier on him. He let the calf loose in the water and it paddled in a fury back to his mother on shore. Once united, the mother and calf ran into the woods.

It had been a long morning. Once we were finished on the island, Trevor came to shore and unloaded the packs of food he had prepared for us. We ate his peanut butter sandwiches with relish, swatting away at the flies that were attacking our necks and ears.

"Well that was interesting," Amy remarked. "What's in

store for tomorrow?"

"Tomorrow, we head to a peninsula. There was a sighting of a mother and calf that I haven't collared yet," replied O'Connell, who by that time had joined us on shore.

"Why do the moose come to an island to calf?" I asked him.

"Islands and peninsulas are the only way to avoid predators. Calf mortality rates here are mostly from bear and wolf predation," he responded.

We sat and contemplated this fact. Tom reached over to hand me another sandwich, with a gesture that said, 'Want another?' I declined, but noted his small gesture of kindness with a look of appreciation. Then we loaded onto the boats to head back to the camp and get ready for tomorrow.

When we got back, I immediately went to the showers, hoping some cold water would subdue the flaring welts left by the flies. I put on my sweatshirt and jeans. There was a chill again as the evening descended. The air smelled of charcoal. I walked into the living area to find a mirror to braid my hair. I always had the habit of French-braiding my hair after a swim or when it was wet. I pulled it back and watched my fingers do their work, and noticed Tom in the reflection, sitting behind me, following my every move. I turned around and smiled at him. He flashed one back. We were both glowing from the day's events. That evening Trevor treated us to a Bar-B-Que dinner that was both spicy and sweet. Ribs, corn, and beans that we ate like it was a last supper. The day's exertions melted away while we sat out by the lake around a campfire Tom had made. As the moon rose in the sky, Trevor told us tales of the park.

"One of our most famous residents was Tom Thomson," he started.

"Who is Tom Thomson," Dan asked.

"I have one of his paintings on a postcard I picked up

at the outpost," I offered.

"Yes, he was a famous artist from Toronto, eh," he continued, nodding at me. "His body was recovered eight days after his boat was found floating upside down. He was only thirty-nine, found at the bottom of Canoe Lake. It was July 1917; my grandmother was here when it happened. She worked as a cook for the Park Ranger back then and she told me stories about Thomson."

"He was more famous after his death than before. He did not make much while he was working, sold a few painting and sketches that's all," O'Connell contributed. He had spent enough time in Algonquin to know the story, but he deferred back to Trevor and went to get more wood for the fire. He had heard this tale before and knew how long it would take.

"So you saw his work then, eh?" Trevor continued his story without waiting, although I opened my mouth to respond. His peculiar habit of ending a sentence in 'eh,' as if it were a question, was just part of his Canadian vernacular.

"It was a July day, like Jim said, and Thompson was staying in the park. He had been here a whole year, trying to sketch and paint the changing seasons. He would camp out in the wilderness as much as he could, or stay at the lodge nearby when the weather was too cold or treacherous. He knew the park well because he had worked as a fire ranger here. But this particular summer, he wanted to just sketch and paint. He put all of his effort into it and didn't want to be disturbed. He was a bit of a recluse my grandmother said, but everyone around here knew him well. My grandmother said the Park Rangers were frantic looking for his body when they discovered his upturned canoe. They scoured the lake, and other areas nearby where they knew he spent most of his time. Wouldn't ya know, eh, his body was discovered by a local fisherman. They dragged the body up and found a bruise over the left eye, some fishing line tangled around his ankles, and that was 'bout it for evidence. They called it an accidental drowning. But the locals never believed that theory. Some say it was murder. A friend owed him money and he had been demanding it back for some time. The night before his death he was in a scuffle about it. My grandmother sided with another story, she always believed it was a suicide. Said he was engaged to a local woman who was pregnant and he just couldn't stand the idea of settling down."

The story sent chills down my spine. The suicide, the pregnancy, sounded hauntingly familiar. I started to shiver. Tom, who was sitting on the log next to me, draped his arms around my shoulders and rubbed them, an intimate gesture he would never dare if Patrice were around. O'Connell came back with more logs for the fire. We sat through the night and watched the crescent moon rise over the water.

In the morning, I was treated to the longing wail of the Common Loon, echoing across the lake. I glanced at my watch: it was 5:30 AM. The kitchen was again filled with the aroma of coffee and some kind of French toast Trevor was making. He grunted a hello to me — he may have been a good story-teller, but he was not much for small talk — as I took a mug of coffee out to the deck. The silhouettes of the spruce trees looked human, and gave the impression of sentries standing guard in the mist. I inhaled the aroma of coffee, equaled only by the smell of the evergreens. The scent stirred a memory of a time years before when my father took my mother and me out to cut our Christmas tree.

It was a cold December day, a week before Christmas, and my father announced we were going to cut our tree that year. We drove for an hour to a tree farm in the country. There was a lot of snow on the ground so my mother had instructed us to dress appropriately. We had on hats and mittens, winter coats and boots. When we arrived I was treated to the sight of miles and miles of evergreen trees planted neatly in rows. My father took his small saw out of the trunk and we proceeded to the barn to ask the owners where to cut.

"We need to ask where the Balsam firs are. Those are the best Christmas trees," my mother insisted. "They have a great fragrance and the needles are not sharp like spruce."

We trudged in the snow, me with a long plastic sled in tow — for what seemed like miles to find a tree that would meet my mother's approval. After my father cut it down we dragged it back to the barn on my sled to be baled. My father struggled to get the large tree on the top of our station wagon. When we finally got it in the house and my father had it firmly planted in the tree stand, he cut the bale wire holding the tree in a bundle, and the tree unfolded in our living room. The smell of Christmas filled the air. The three of us sat on the couch with a cup of hot cocoa, admiring the tree and taking in that wonderful evergreen scent.

Tom came out on the deck and disturbed my reminiscing. I didn't mind though.

"Did you hear that Loon this morning?" he asked.

I looked out at Lake Sasajewun to determine where the sound of the Loon came from. "Yes." I smiled. "It's a wonderful alarm clock." He sat down with his coffee.

"You can get used to it here, the quiet, solitude. When it's time to leave you regret going back to civilization," he said.

"I could see that." I glanced over at him, his hair was tangled from the night of sleep, his eyes were clear and blue. He took a sip of his coffee, looked over at me and smiled. Embarrassed to be staring at him, I looked away quickly. "You would miss Patrice though."

"Not so sure about that," he said. That was unexpected, but admittedly, I liked his response.

He looked down at my feet, I had wool socks on to protect against the morning chill.

"How are your feet doing with those new hiking boots?"

I winced. In the morning glow I had tried to forget the pain.

"Great; just a little blistered."

"Did you do what I told you to break them in?"

"Yes." I lied. He had told me to purchase the boots well in advance so that I could break them in. In reality I had bought them the night before we left, put them on and sauntered around the suite for a couple of hours. My feet were suffering as a result.

Just then the Loon gave off its call, "Where are you?" it seemed to say into the fog, as if it had lost its mate. A look of acknowledgement passed between us, the slightest clue that deep inside we knew what it was trying to say.

This day's tracking turned out to be a bit trickier. We had to find the mother and calf on the peninsula without the help of telemetry. Park officials had told O'Connell that they spotted a mother and calf in this area but we weren't sure where they were, so we had a lot of tracking to do. We drove about an hour to the calving spot. We started on the far end of the peninsula, at its widest point of land. We spread out in the same manner as the day before and worked our way to the end of the point. O'Connell was on land with us, Trevor in the boat offshore. O'Connell needed to tag and collar both the mother and calf today so he had his dart gun with tranquilizer.

We worked our way through the woods. The fog was starting to clear but the air felt dense. It seemed as though the fog suppressed the birds' chatter; the woods were quiet all morning. We fanned out as we had the day before, each with a radio. The forest consisted of conifers, but there were a few aspen sprinkled throughout. Tracking was tough. Forging ahead we had to circumnavigate large spruce trees and I had no idea if we were actually in a straight line by the time we were all in position. My feet were killing me in the new boots.

After what seemed like hours, we reached the end of the peninsula. My feet were throbbing. I could see Trevor and the boat offshore, and the calf and mother swimming away from him and back to land. I heard O'Connell on the radio call out, "She's running. Back on land, she's madder than hell; find a tree!" I couldn't see anyone from where I was standing, the dark, dense spruce trees blocking my view. I looked for, and found, a wide tree to huddle behind and hoped everyone else found the same. We heard a loud scream coming from somewhere near the shore, it was Bridget, the pregnant woman. That got us all out of hiding. One by one we arrived at the beach to see the moose racing in circles from O'Connell, to Tom, to Bridget, who was cowering behind a very thin aspen. O'Connell raised his rifle and aimed for the rear-end of the moose. He pulled the trigger and the dart distributed a shot of carfentanil citrate, mixed with xylazine hydrochloride — potent tranquilizing agents. She staggered for a few minutes, and went down.

While Amy and I calmed Bridget, the others got to work. The calf was mewing its discontent, but stayed near the mother. O'Connell took out needles from his pack he had been carrying, drew some blood from the huge jugular vein into a vial, and handed it to Liz who secured it for blood serum analysis at the hospital lab. Tom took out a stethoscope and kept track of her heart rate. O'Connell drew the mouth open to examine her teeth and determine age. Liz helped him measure the girth of the neck. He then collared her, punched a tag in her ear, and injected her with antibiotics to ensure she did not get infection from any injuries sustained during the capture.

Tom motioned to me to come over to him. By then, Bridget, Amy and I had moved to be near the calf. He was sitting quietly, his heart racing, waiting for his mother to be released. One could not help but feel sorry for the animal, even if all of this was for the benefit of understanding calf mortality rates. I left my spot beside Amy and Bridget, and sat down next to Tom.

He placed my hand over the animal's enormous chest so I could feel the same thing he was feeling: the up and down movement of its breathing and strong heart-beat. We looked at each other, feeling the pulse of this magnificent creature, and shared a moment of awe.

O'Connell injected the reversal agent into her veins and within five minutes she clambered onto her feet, languidly shook her great body, and swayed around looking for her calf. Instinctively, the calf knew to go to her and they trotted off together into the woods.

After that event O'Connell decided a break was needed before his volunteers mutinied. We took the next day off to swim and relax on Opeongo Lake. Trevor and O'Connell brought us by boat to the south arm of the lake. There were large granite outcroppings, ledges where we could light a fire and enjoy the views. A few brave ones, like me, took a dip in the lake. It was frigid: bone-chilling. Tom and I swam together, while the others stayed on shore. He, like me, was a strong swimmer.

"We owned a pond, spring fed. It was usually colder than this," he said. I did not last long in the water. We took a short hike in the woods, much to my chagrin, although I was able to use my sandals for this walk and the cold water had numbed my blisters to the point of no feeling. O'Connell was pointing out various specimens of herbaceous plants and shrubs that moose liked to eat, and clearings of aspens where the beaver were building dams.

True to form, Trevor was a folklorist of the woods. He knew more about the natural history of trees than anyone I had ever encountered. I asked him where he obtained his knowledge, thinking he had spent time at some university in Canada.

"No, tried that; didn't work for me," was all he said.

Dan pointed to one of the spruces, "What kind of pine tree is that?" he asked Trevor. I smiled at his mistake. People commonly call all evergreens pine trees.

"That, my friend, is not a pine, but a spruce. Look over there," he pointed to a towering white pine.

"That is a pine; the White pine. Colonists in your country used to get into skirmishes with the Crown over those trees. They were highly valued as masts for the British Navy. The Brits didn't want the colonists to cut them down for their own uses. Some say it led to a revolution, eh?" he winked at us.

Bridget was staring at the trembling aspen, their leaves shaking like shiny earrings on a woman.

"And those trees with the whitish-gray bark, what are those?" she asked.

"Those are aspen. When you come across a large grove of aspen you can see the trees talking to each other, like one large extended family, that clones itself underground."

We pondered this interpretation of the aspen-grove. It seemed almost feasible that they were talking to each other.

We found a good spot on a granite ledge to start a campfire and cook a late lunch. The view was spectacular. In the middle of the lake was an island, "Bates Island," Tom pointed it out to me. "That is where the bear attacked some campers about a decade ago."

It did not take long for us to hear the story from Trevor. We were sitting around the campfire, Tom and I sitting close together, trying to rid ourselves of the chill from the afternoon swim in Opeongo, when Trevor started in on the story of the bear that attacked and consumed a couple from Toronto. As soon as he began, O'Connell got up to replenish the fire with more wood.

"You know," he looked down at Trevor, "you really are a party-killer." He turned to us. "My wife hates this story," he warned.

Looking for moral support, Trevor looked over at

Tom. "You know this story, eh?"

Tom held up his hands in a shrug, "I hardly remember since you last told it," he said to Trevor and to the crowd. We all turned our attention to Trevor.

"It was the Canadian holiday weekend in October '91, eh?" He looked out for Jim, but Jim was not there to back him up. "Jim and I received a call from the Ranger. A family member had phoned the station to alert the Ranger that the couple, both in their late thirties, hadn't come back from a long weekend of camping. He asked us to check on Bates Island while we were out on our rounds checking the telemetry units. When we reached the shore we knew something was wrong, the ground was covered in blood and there were bear tracks everywhere. There were various articles of clothing and other items scattered about the campsite. Their canoe was all tied up in many knots; it would have taken them awhile to untie it to escape. One oar was snapped in half, and there was a can of lighter fluid and a lighter. We also found the guy's glasses and an empty can of Dinty Moore Stew; the cooking pan was licked clean. Only one air mattress had been blown-up. We figured they hadn't even finished setting up camp when the bear arrived." He shivered for a minute, poked the fire and continued. I looked around for O'Connell but he was nowhere close by.

"We followed the trail of blood. Jim and I were a bit scared by it, but we figured whatever had happened to the couple was days before so, if it was a bear attack the thing would be long gone, eh? Along the trail of blood we saw piles of leaves with bits and pieces of blood-stained clothing, places where the bear had dragged the bodies, then stopped to cover them up while it took breaks. Still, there were no signs of the bodies yet. Then we came up to a knoll, and there it was — a 300-pound she-bear, guarding the corpses, or what was left of them. I saw a flash of red hair, the woman, and the man — he still had his boots on, and I remember thinking that was odd. The bear gave off a 'woof', a warning to us to stay away, then it ran off into the woods."

We were speechless, all of us looking out at the island across the lake and looking around for signs of bear. I got closer to Tom. By then O'Connell had come back.

"Finished with the story yet?" he turned to Trevor. Trevor shook his head.

"So what happened to the bear?" Amy asked, wondering what we all were. Was it still roaming these woods? O'Connell continued the story, assuring us there was no hungry bear waiting to attack. He did not want us bailing on him in the middle of his research.

"We called the ranger station and they sent out some men. We fanned out on the island with shotguns and left two in a boat off-shore in case the bear decided to swim for it. The spruce was so thick on that island we could hardly see in front of us. I was worried someone would mistake me for the bear and shoot by accident. I was standing in a thicket of trees when I heard a shot go off, and someone radioed that they got the bear. We dragged it to shore, put it in my boat and I took it back to the station. It was eventually carted off to a lab where they gutted it to make sure it was the bear that had killed the couple, and sure enough, there was enough content in its stomach to prove it was."

"So what made the bear do that, you know, eat the people? I thought bears ate moose calves and berries?" Lisa questioned him.

"It's highly unusual for a bear to attack unprovoked and guard its prey. We think maybe it was the time of year. October is a time bears are storing up food for the winter. Who knows, maybe the campfire and food is what lured it in," O'Connell answered her.

"I'll never forget though, the look on her face. When we came upon their bodies, her eyes were open and she had this look of terror. The bear had stripped the bodies clean of the fat. She had a wristwatch on and it was still on her arm though there was nothing else left but bone," Jim looked shaken, recalling the events.

"We determined they died quickly, if that is any consolation, a single blow to the neck. We think the bear went after her first, while she was cooking, and the man tried to fight the bear off with his oar, and then maybe tried to light it on fire with his can of fuel. The bear turned on the man, after killing the woman. When they were both dead, it started eating their flesh, and when it felt threatened by passing boats, or fisherman, it must have started dragging the bodies away from the shore and campsite," Trevor ended the story for O'Connell.

We all sat silently, thinking of the man and woman from Toronto, getting away for a weekend into the wilderness to try and forget the deadlines, the meetings, the phone calls they needed to make, and soak in the beauty of this place, only to be confronted by the terror of an animal that could not be stopped.

"Told you it was a party killer," O'Connell looked at Trevor accusingly. Trevor shrugged. Story telling is what he did.

Liz, the lemur lady, took hold of my elbow as we were packing up the site to leave, "Let's hit the Outpost store and buy some bear mace," she said.

I nodded in agreement. If this woman, who had spent months in the jungles of Madagascar was scared, then I was too. I was also thinking of the young couple from the Outpost who had bummed a ride from O'Connell; someone needed to warn them to get the hell out of the woods before October.

On the way back to the camp, Tom, Liz and I stopped at the Outpost. Tom picked up some supplies for O'Connell, and I wandered around the store with Liz looking for the mace. Tom came up to us when we were standing in front of the display of poster replicas of Tom Thomson's work.

We all looked up at the eerily desolate pictures of the Park.

"He must have spent a lot of time here to be able to capture all of these images on canvas," Liz said.

He had a way of stripping out all the background noise from a scene so that what you saw was the raw beauty of the place. One picture could have been taken from the deck at the base camp, a scene of a lake, the sky a yellow haze, the water a reflection of the yellow. The mountains were a silhouette in the background, with a small dusting of snow, the only indication it may have been spring, and then an ink-black outline of a tree in the foreground, a pine of some sort.

"His pictures reflect his comfort in isolation," Tom said. We all nodded in agreement.

We were halfway back to the camp when I realized I never mailed my postcard to Stuart. It was still ensconced in my pack.

That night after dinner Tom, O'Connell and I were sitting around the fireplace, Tom and O'Connell discussing the equipment and other medical devices needed for the research. I took off my socks to examine my sore feet. Tom saw me wince when I took off my socks.

"Let me see," he said, as he grabbed my feet and placed them on his lap. A mixture of pain and pleasure tingled up my leg and to my groin when he touched my feet. My blisters had broken open, and were rubbed raw.

"Ouch," O'Connell said, "that doesn't look good."

I managed a smile, "I'm getting used to my new boots."

"Well, you can take another day off tomorrow. Trevor, Liz and I need to check out a few locations for moose with collars, and Bridget, Dan and Amy are heading home anyway. A new group is coming in from the college," he looked over at Tom. "You remember Steve Milne? He is bringing a bunch of undergraduates with him."

Tom nodded, "It will be good to see him again."

The Loon woke me up again, proving to be a reliable alarm clock. I looked at my watch; 5:30 AM exactly. That day we said our good-byes to Bridget, Dan and Amy, the threat of man-eating bears and stampeding moose proving to be too much for Bridget. I couldn't blame her for wanting to exit early.

While some went to scout locations, the rest of us went out on the Algonquin canoes that had been beckoning us from the beach since the day we arrived. We set out mid-morning. It was going to be a hot, sunny day. The fog had lifted early and the sun was beating down on the lake. We all had our sunglasses on to avoid the glare. As we paddled along the shoreline, we saw the two mating Loons about 100 yards away, their sleek black silhouette strikingly serene against the early morning sun.

"Why is it that I never see Loons on Canandaigua Lake?" I asked Lisa.

"You might see them when they migrate in the fall, but when they're mating and nesting, they like to have the lake to themselves. Canandaigua may be too busy and crowded for them."

One of the pair dove into the water and we all watched with bated breath for it to resurface. We paddled closer and Lisa suggested we play a game: who could guess where the Loons would resurface, and how long would they be under water. Lisa had an advantage on us. I wrongly guessed four minutes, Tom was closer to the truth at two, and Connor was clueless. The pair entertained us for a long time, diving and resurfacing; on average spending one minute under the water. Lisa, of course, won the game. Watching the Loons kept us entertained for about two hours.

While canoeing, we found a rock ledge near the camp that looked like a good perch to view the sunset. Tom and I made a note to come back to the spot later. When we got back to camp we were all famished. We raided the kitchen and made sandwiches, taking them out on the deck to eat.

Connor and Lisa took off afterwards to the Outpost store. They never made the trip the day before so I let them borrow my car. It was just Tom and me on the deck. We looked out over the water and he placed his hand on top of mine, an intimate gesture I didn't mind.

I looked over at him, "This has been a wonderful experience so far," I said.

"Yes," he sighed, "I am not sure I want to go back."

"At some point Tom, you have to face the music." I think he caught my meaning.

"I know; are you feeling it too?"

"What?"

"Us," he said, "are you feeling a connection?" And then I saw it, that same gaze that Stuart gave me that summer. It was in his eyes, a look of longing, and a question, a look that meant, is this right?

I took a moment to think, "Yes, but it would be unfair to Patrice if anything were to happen between us here."

Just then O'Connell and his crew came back from their outing. Tom took his hand off mine to greet them. I stayed on the deck, rattled by his admission of feelings towards me. The beauty of this place would make anyone feel more alive. What would happen once we got back to Buffalo? I was reminded of what Stuart once said to me when I made the same confession to him three summers ago, god, it seemed like decades. "It's not me that makes you feel so good, it is this place," he had said to me that fateful night when we watched the moon rise and fall.

The undergrads piled out of their van later that afternoon. It was hard to believe I was only a few years older than they were. Was I once so immature? There were three of them in tow with Steve — Tom and O'Connell's friend and colleague. Steve was also a professor at the College of Environmental Science and Forestry in Syracuse. Tom helped him unload his gear as the undergrads oohed and awed all over the place. Their presence brought a renewed energy to all of us the next day as we set out on another trek in the woods, to an island site that O'Connell had located with his telemetry unit where a cow had given birth to a calf.

When we got to the spot, I was determined to anchor the end of the line. The less hiking, the better for me and my blisters, 'Let the undergrads bushwack today,' I thought. A petite blonde was enamored with Tom, following him around wherever we were.

"Here," I said to her, "take this with you. You may need it for the bears." I handed her my mace.

She looked startled. "There are bears in the woods here?" she asked.

I solemnly nodded my head.

"OK, well, I am not going to go in too far from the road then," she declared. We buddied up after that and she stayed away from Tom who was leading the rest of the undergrads deep in the woods.

We followed the same routine for the next few days, the undergrads showing amazing stamina, staying up by the campfire well after midnight and still being able to get up early the next morning. Tom and I met every morning for coffee on the deck and to listen for the Loons. I enjoyed those quiet mornings like nothing else in the world.

After awhile, the undergrads were getting restless. A slight mishap on a return trip convinced Steve and O'Connell to get them out of the woods for a bit, just to get their ya-yahs out. We were unloading the truck after a day in the field.

O'Connell looked over at me as I was about to grab a bag and said, "Let the undergrads do this."

They clambered out of the van and started hauling the equipment out of the truck, laughing about it the whole time. One of the guys grabbed the medical bag and swung it over to a giggling brunette — her shorts were too small, and I could tell by the welts that the bugs had been feasting on her legs all day. She obviously did not read the memo on proper field attire. Thousands of dollars worth of medical equipment went airborne. She caught it, barely, and O'Connell took it from her.

"I'll take that," he said and gently wrested it from her hands. He looked over at Steve and rolled his eyes.

Steve yelled, "OK guys, let's be more careful when unloading the equipment."

That night, they took the undergrads to the nearest town, miles away, to get some subs. Liz, Connor and Lisa made plans as well with my car, and Tom and I took the opportunity to see the sunset on the rock ledge we had spotted. It was a quiet evening without everyone around. We paddled out to the ledge, disembarked and climbed on top to watch the last rays of the sun. Then we went back to camp to wait for the others. As we pulled into the camp, I was overcome with the feeling that this may not last, this wonderful experience I was having with Tom. He must have felt the same. He took my hand as I was getting out of the canoe, held me close to him, and kissed me.

All kinds of feelings flooded through me then but mostly the thought, 'What am I going to do? Should I wait, like the kid in the marshmallow experiment? If I waited for Tom, maybe then he could go back and break things gently with Patrice, allow her to heal and then we could be together without any guilt or worry. Or should I take the chance now, that things would work themselves out? When was the time ever right to begin a relationship? I had waited for Stuart, was still waiting, and where had it gotten me?'

I wasn't going to wait anymore. 'To hell with timing, to hell with Patrice,' I thought. 'This just feels right.' And we walked together into the camp, and into his room. We made love like we had known each other's bodies for years, like a married couple, everything about him seemed so familiar to me.

In the morning, I did not want to be seen coming out of his room, but we must have slept through the Loon calls because when we woke, it was already seven AM. I put on my clothes and opened his door quietly, sneaking into the hallway to my room at the other end. As I was leaving I bumped into the petite blonde undergrad.

"Oh, excuse me," I said. She looked at me, disheveled and wearing the same clothes as the night before, and glanced down the hall from where I had come.

"Oh! Sorry," she said embarrassed.

We tried to be discrete, but after awhile it became obvious to everyone that Tom and I were together. We were quietly murmuring to each other over dinner one night when O'Connell looked over at us, and with that twinkle in his eye, said something like, "Enjoying yourselves aren't ya?"

We spent the next three nights together after our field-work, and tried not to think about when it would be time to leave.

The long drive home from Algonquin was difficult for us both. We were in mourning, not only because we had to leave, but also from thinking about what we had to face when we got back. I dropped him off at his apartment, he kissed me good-bye with a sad smile. We didn't want to talk about what would happen next. It really was all up to him. When I walked into my suite I was confronted by Patrice, the look on her face made me drop my bags, she looked like she had received some terrible news. Had Tom been able to reach her so quickly?

I was about to stammer out an apology when she ran to me, gave me a big hug, and said, "I am so sorry!"

I was confused. Why was she sorry? She should be mad at me.

Just then Julie and Sue came out of the kitchen. Patrice was sobbing; Julie put her hand on my shoulder, "It's your Aunt. We tried to reach you but your cell phone wasn't connecting. I'm sorry Emalee; she died yesterday."

- Part Five Canandaigua-

CHAPTER SIXTEEN

They say you can't return, and in a way they are right. Oh, you can come back to the ancestral coordinates, but the latitude and longitude are about the only things that remain the same. — John A. Weeks

She died while sailing.

"It was a heart attack," Karl told me when I arrived at the camp. I couldn't keep track of the days or the time. I remembered being led to my bed, Julie giving me an Ambien, and Tom by my side. Tom insisted on driving me to my camp with my car. He left me with Karl and promised he'd be back. Someone followed us and drove him back to campus. Karl and I were in the kitchen the morning after I arrived, still in a daze. His daughter Mary was there, catering to our every need; when I sat down she placed a mug of coffee in front of me.

"She went out for a sail in the morning. I was at the store in town. She hadn't shown any signs of feeling ill. The doctors think it happened suddenly. She didn't have time to react. When I came back I saw her sunfish out in the water and I thought it was odd that it wasn't moving, that I couldn't see Audrey. I took my motor-boat out and found her. She had her life jacket on, but it was too late."

He finished the story and let out a big sigh, so much sadness in his voice. "I just wish I could have been there for her, you know?"

"Karl," I said, as I reached for his hand, "there was nothing you could have done, and she was where she wanted to be, died where she wanted to die — on the lake."

Audrey had made her wishes clear. She was cremated, and we were to scatter her ashes in the lake. A few days later Karl and I trudged out to his small motor-boat. I looked out on the water. A few hundred yards offshore were several sailboats, their sails facing the wind, their movements still. Others were sailing out to join the crowd that was forming; they were my Aunt's sailing friends. We puttered out in Karl's small boat to join the rag-tag group of Audrey's friends, the passengers of the sailboats waving at us forlornly. I recognized the childhood friends she had known for her seventy-three years at the lake, some of our neighbors, and people from the lake association. Karl stopped at the edge of the contingent. Silently, I took her ashes, stood at the stern of the boat and let them fly in the wind.

I stayed at the lake, not wanting to go back to campus, not sure of what I would do when I got there. I was not motivated to do my research or to take classes, I just wanted to sit on the screened-in porch and stare out at the lake. Tom called me every night. He broke up with Patrice, but he did not have the heart to tell her about us. He thought it best to wait, saying there was no reason to cause me or her more angst. I was glad.

Karl and I spent a lot of time just sitting, reading condolence letters from Audrey's myriad of friends. Mary was a godsend; she cooked, cleaned, screened our phone calls. One day she came out to the porch and said to Karl, "I think it's time you told her."

I looked over at him, not sure what she meant. Karl

slowly got up from his chair. He had aged quite a lot since Audrey's death. He took a large envelope from the desk in the living room, brought it to me, and placed it on my lap.

"You need to read this," he said.

I opened it up. The letterhead was from a legal firm in Rochester. I read the first three lines, something about a lawsuit against the pharmaceutical company, my father, his death, class action, unwarranted, legal terms I did not understand.

I turned to Karl, "What is this?"

"Audrey and I filed a lawsuit on your behalf when you lost your parents. We sued the pharmaceutical company that made the drug your father was on when he, well when it happened. The claim was just recently recognized, and settled."

I looked back at the paper, towards the bottom was the settlement amount, a staggering sum of money.

"What am I supposed to do with this?" I asked.

"Whatever you want," he replied.

If I had had more time, and less stress, to process the information, I may not have put it away so quickly. But Audrey's death and the settlement were too much to take in at the moment. I put the envelope back in the desk to think about later. The next day when Karl said he was heading over to the Marina to meet with some people, I asked him to take me along. I needed to get out. We took his new car, he had retired the motorcycle after the landslide at his camp.

There were a few Amish gentlemen in the Marina parking lot, standing next to another man who looked out of place in his dark blue suit and tie. Karl pulled up in his car, got out and greeted the men. He made quick introductions around and then said we needed to wait for one other. I stood over to the side, trying not to pry. Then I saw him walking towards us from the direction of the Lowell's house. His tall stature and wavy straw-colored hair were so recognizable to me as he came closer.

I was about to call out his name, when suddenly Karl waved to him and said, "Ben, over here."

It was Stuart's older brother Ben. He must have had some business with these men. He came up to the group and shook everyone's hands. Karl introduced him to me. "Yes, I know you, Emalee, you were friends with my brother Stuart? I am so sorry to hear about your Aunt. My family offers its condolences."

"Thanks," I murmured. Except for their age difference -— Ben looked a decade older than Stuart —- they looked a lot alike, even had the same mannerisms, voice inflection, and eye color, which I could never quite pin down.

A sudden depression washed over me. I left the men to see the vineyards across the road and I followed the same path Stuart and I took three years before. I wished I had asked Ben about Stuart but it didn't seem like the right time to get too familiar. The Amish men, working on the vines, were wearing plain blue shirts, rolled up at the sleeves, black overalls, and flat-brimmed, straw hats. They looked over at me walking and waved. I ended up at the rock. The view was the same, but everything else was different.

We got back into the car, the men calling out their good-byes in recognition of a meeting that went well. I asked Karl what was going on.

"Well, the Amish want to go into a partnership with Ben Lowell. They want to buy the marina from the developers, and Ben wants to operate it. They plan to build a winery where tourists can pull up on their boats, sample the wine and eat local food grown by the Amish. They even think there may be a market in weddings and other events."

"So who was the gentleman with the suit?"

"He represents the Finger Lakes Land Trust, Ben Lowell and the Amish want to put an easement on the land, keeping it out of development in perpetuity. The only buildings allowed would be the marina, which is already there, and the winery." It was the first time in days that Karl looked happy. He had done it, saved a precious piece of open space on the lake. Audrey would have been proud of him.

The next morning Mary came into my room to wake me, "Claire is here to see you," she said. I was groggy from sleep. I had been dreaming about Stuart showing up on a boat. Was that what I heard just minutes before Mary woke me, the sound of a small motor on the water? I brushed my teeth, went down the stairs and saw Claire, sitting on the porch. She rose and gave me a big hug. "I am so sorry," she said. We looked each other over. She had cut her long hair short, and looked more cosmopolitan than when we had last seen each other.

"How is New York?"

She laughed, "Fabulous!"

"And Peter? I hear he is famous." He was the elephant in the room, I had not seen him since I was back. His mother had come by with a casserole, our refrigerator was full of them, and told me he was nationally known for his artwork now.

"Oh yes, he is indeed becoming famous," she said. "He has many patrons who just adore his work." She had a hint of sarcasm in her voice, or was it resentment I was hearing?

"He's sold a few of his paintings and is now doing interior design. He was always one for making something out of nothing in an empty room." I knew that well.

"Sounds as if you're jealous," I was learning to be blunt; when time is so short, why not just get to the point? "How is your writing coming along?" I said.

"Well let's just say that since the day we arrived in New York it has been all about Peter. That does not leave me with much," she said.

"I'm sorry to hear that. You're talented too," I said. "You shouldn't let Peter's fame get in the way of your dreams."

She scoffed at that. "I can handle Peter's self-absorption, his outlandish project ideas, but one thing I cannot bear, is his indifference to my gender." She looked at me then to see if I was registering her meaning. I did not understand.

"What do you mean?"

"I mean that Peter has many patrons, both male and female and they all adore him," she said.

I thought for a moment, and then responded, "You mean Peter is bisexual?" I was incredulous. How could I have missed that after all of these years of friendship?

"I can't believe you never knew," she stared out at the water.

"Did you know when you met him?" I asked.

"Of course, but like a fool I thought I could change him." She quaffed the coffee Mary had so graciously left on the porch side table.

"For someone who is so observant of everything around her, you are a poor observer of human behavior. Or maybe it's just that you see what you want to see in people and nothing more. Either way, it works for you. I myself couldn't deal with it anymore. I left him, although we remain friends," she said.

She said good-bye. She was staying for a few days at her parents' camp, and would try to stop over again before she went back to New York.

"Peter should be here in a few days," she said, taking my hands as she was leaving. "He wanted to come right away but he had a show to do. He told me to tell you how sorry he is, and that he will come to see you as soon as possible."

I felt so sorry for her, for them both, for all of us. I knew that our friendships would never be the same.

There was no way for me to verify with Peter what Claire had told me. It was not as if I could just call him out of the blue in New York and say, "Hey Peter, are you bi?" I wondered if Audrey and Karl knew. I decided to ask Karl later that morning.

"I'm not surprised," he said, "we've all suspected for years. I rather think Claire was a distraction for him. He's more likely homosexual and just finally admitting it to himself."

Now I knew why Audrey never worried about me when I was with Peter, staying at his house overnight, spending countless hours with him; why Peter needed me when we were younger to counteract any peer ridicule he might encounter from friends who knew deep inside what he was hiding. It was then that I started to piece together our relationship. It all started to make sense to me that we never became lovers. Peter would never hurt me that way, not when he knew he could not fulfill his commitment to me. He would never lead me on. Why he did this to Claire, I was not sure. Maybe like me, he needed someone to believe in him, and help him get his work accomplished. Maybe as I had used Toby for companionship and to help me with my research, he used Claire to get started in New York. I was sure he loved her, but he knew that was never going to be enough for Claire.

My days were lazy. It was late June and I still had no plans, and I didn't care. I would get up late in the morning, not even noticing the time, sit and drink coffee on the porch watching the boats go by on the lake, and barely move from that position except to take a shower or swim in the lake. The nights were still cool, the lake cold, and it felt good to swim in the cold water, if only to feel something. I was numb with grief. I had to make a decision about what to do with the settlement money. One day Karl broached the subject while sipping our coffee — we were left to ourselves to make it now. Mary had to get back to her family.

His eyes filled with grief, he looked at me seriously, "Emalee, you have to start making some decisions."

I was after all, the last of the Rawlings. This camp, my Aunt's house in Rochester, they were all mine now, and I didn't know what to do with all of the responsibility. I did know one thing though.

"Karl, if you would like to, and I think you would, I want you to stay here. I don't want to sell this camp, and I can't keep up with it, not at this point in my life. I am only half-way through a PhD."

He nodded. "OK, I would like to stay, this place holds so many good memories for me," he said. "And what about the money?"

"I want to use it to keep this camp. There is enough there to pay the taxes for a very long time. And Audrey had an ongoing list of things that needed repair, the roof, the siding, the steps to the lake. I am sure we can put that money to good use. Would you take care of that for me?"

He patted my hand, "Of course I will. We will work it all out."

So that was settled, I did not have to think anymore about the money. I was glad for it: the money was just a reminder of all that I had lost anyway. My father and Audrey would want it put back into the camp, to keep it going for the next generation, if there was to be one. We sat looking out on the water, the lake was calm and still that morning, a small motor boat came puttering up to our dock. I saw his brown head and ran out to greet him in my pajamas. It was Peter.

After our greetings, and Peter's condolences, I ran up to change. Peter wanted to take me on the boat somewhere. As much as he had changed from New York, nothing had changed between us. He was the same old Peter. To me, Peter was like an old habit, I could continue where I left off. He drove me to the old boathouse, the source of his dreams. We idled into the one open bay and sat in the cavernous structure.

"It's mine now," he beamed at me.

"What?" I could not believe it.

"I got some investors to go in on it and we bought it from the Town. They wanted to unload it and the group that was trying to save it just could not raise the money needed. They didn't mind when they heard our plans."

"So you are going to turn it into an art gallery?"

"Yes. I want to promote local artists and craftsmen. There is a lot for parking up above, and we can put in a few slips for people to arrive by water. We're hoping the local cruise boat will make this a stop as well. I think it will work." He looked around at the place with a hunger in his eyes, already changing things, retrofitting the woodwork, the bays, the loft.

I looked around with him. I could see it now as well. "Peter, I am so happy for you."

Things were falling into place for everyone at the lake. Peter had his boathouse, Karl had his way with the developers of the marina, and I had the security of knowing that the camp would be here for the rest of my life. Tom called almost everyday asking when I would be back. He was planning to visit the coming weekend, which would be a good excuse for me to take him out on the lake and get me out of my doldrums. I was looking forward to his visit.

On the Wednesday before Tom's visit there was a gathering of the friends' of the lake association at Thendara to celebrate saving the marina from development. Karl invited me to come with him, and since I hadn't been out much, I thought it was as good an excuse as any to put on some make-up and act human.

To my surprise, Dave was still a bartender. He was

friendly with me, offering his sympathy and getting me a drink on the house. I sat at the bar with him, feeling a bit nervous to be back. I looked around. Nothing much had changed. Dave and I shared a few laughs about the patrons and he seemed more relaxed than he was a few summers ago. He said he had bought a house in town and was settling down with a woman, someone I did not know. The regulars at the bar loved him; he had his place here.

Karl waved me to follow him to the terrace so I left Dave at the bar and proceeded out. We both made small talk to a number of Audrey's old friends, "Yes, I'm getting a PhD." "Yes it's in aquatic science." "Yes, I may just move back."

We endured the well-meaning and relentless reminders of Audrey and how much she meant to everyone, including me. "Audrey was my dear friend, I still have the sea glass wreath she made me. You must miss her." "I miss seeing Audrey on the lake on her sunfish." "You look just like her."

I was exhausted by this exchange and was ready to leave when I noticed Ben Lowell speaking with a young woman across the room. She was about my age. She had long dark hair and looked strikingly like Danielle. I had to do a double take, thinking my mind must be playing tricks on me. Ben saw me looking at them. She looked my way as well. That is when I realized it was clearly not Danielle — this woman smiled at me. Ben proceeded to walk towards me. When he was halfway across the floor, my mind registered that it was not Ben approaching, but Stuart.

He came up to me, reached down, held my arms, and brushed a kiss on the side of my face. I shuddered at his touch.

"Hello Emalee," he whispered in my ear.

I was in a daze, why hadn't Karl told me Stuart was here? "Hello Stuart."

"How are you?"

A loaded question everyone was asking me. I wanted to say 'Despondent, longing for Tom to arrive; thrilled to see you finally.'

"I'm fine." I lied.

He looked me over not really believing it. "Emalee, I wanted to…"

"Well if it isn't Stuart Lowell!" A man I didn't recognize interrupted. He leaned into Stuart, shook his hand; clearly on the brink of intoxication.

He looked up at me with his ruddy face and said, "And Emalee Rawlings! I'm so sorry to hear about your Aunt."

"Yes," was all that I could muster. The man looked at us both and realized he had interrupted something of importance.

"Well, I will talk to you later Stuart," he slapped him on the back, "and congratulations on the engagement."

Stuart grunted a vague thank you, and guiltily glanced my way. All of the blood in my head went south. The room was spinning; the dark haired woman that looked like a smiling Danielle was working her way towards us. I had to get out of there.

I staggered towards the exit, Karl took hold of my arm, "What's wrong?" He scanned the room and saw Stuart next to his fiancée. He nodded to me, "Do you want me to take you home?'

"No, I will walk. Thanks Karl." I left.

It was dusk now, the sun was setting, the lake shimmering in its glow. The air was fresh, the wind was picking up, my head started to clear while I walked. Half-way to the camp I passed the path I used to bike down to watch the sunset. It was a black asphalt drive now, two stone pillars stood at the entranceway; down the driveway I could see a huge house, blocking the view of the sunset for anyone but the owner, their little piece of paradise.

Just then Stuart pulled up in his car, and rolled down the passenger window, "Get in," he directed me.

For the past three years I would often conjure his image and the thing I could never quite remember was his eye color. Was it blue, gray, green or brown? Who was it that said, eyes are the 'window to the soul?' If that was the case, I never got a decent view. I looked into his eyes and noted that they were hazel; they changed color depending on the lighting — no wonder I could never tell. That day they looked green. I got into his car.

We didn't speak as he drove me back to my camp. When he pulled into my driveway, he parked the car and turned off the ignition. We sat there in silence.

Finally I asked him, "Where is your fiancée? Isn't she wondering why you chased after me?"

"Her name is Deidre. I told her you were distraught about Audrey and I wanted to make sure you got home ok. I'm sorry to hear about Audrey, I went to the Thendara celebration to look for you. Be honest with me, how are you holding up?"

I sighed, "Not that great. But Tom, my friend is coming to visit this weekend, he will make things better." I hoped this information hurt him.

"Well thanks for the ride." I opened the door of the car and ran towards the house before he could see me cry. He followed me into the camp.

I went to the refrigerator to get a cold drink, not offering one to Stuart.

"Let's go to the porch and talk," he said.

We walked out to the porch and sat in the rocking chairs, looking out at the familiar landscape, one we had shared quite often that summer three years ago. It seemed like eternity before either of us spoke, and then he broke the silence.

"You shouldn't have left that morning."

"Really Stuart? That's all you have to say after three years? And what was I supposed to do? I saw the whole thing between you and Danielle, whatever that was. It sounded like she was practically begging you. Was she pregnant with your child?"

He flinched. I don't think he expected me to accuse him of that.

"No." he said quietly. "Danielle was sick. I'm not sure who the father was, I would guess Dave, she was hanging around him all summer."

"And you never told me about her all summer. She kept following us around and you never thought to tell me what was wrong with her; that you two were so close; that she was jealous? Not that I couldn't see that, but I never understood why. Stuart, she was obsessed with you," I said in disgust. "And because of that, we never had a chance to be in love with each other the way I wanted so desperately to be."

"It's not that I didn't think of you in that way, but I didn't want to hurt you."

I softened a bit, my anger at him was melting.

"I couldn't follow-through with my feelings for you," he continued. "It wouldn't have been fair to you, not when I was so conflicted. You have to understand something Emalee. Danielle was my soul-mate since we were young. I loved her. But she changed: something happened to her, I'm not sure what, but she was on some pretty heavy medication by the time she was sixteen. I then became her protector, her shield from everything. It was an exhausting job. I couldn't keep up with it, with her. When you came along it was like a release for me from my responsibility to her. I finally had someone else to care about."

He paused. "She hated you for it."

The air suddenly seemed chilly and I shivered.

"And Emalee, it's not like you led me to believe that there was something more to what we had. You only once mentioned how you felt towards me and you never said you loved me, just that you felt 'good' around me or something strange like that."

I looked at him, what had he expected from me? A full

confession of my feelings? To allow myself to be that vulnerable was not like me, not now, not then, well maybe now. Maybe I had changed. But it was all too late for us.

"When you left I felt awful. I wanted to explain everything to you. I tried to call but Audrey said you were sleeping. I had to go to work that day, of all days, and fix someone's boat. I figured I would come to your camp afterwards. By that afternoon though, I got a phone call from my Aunt. She was frantic. She and Danielle had an agreement that Danielle would check in once a week and she hadn't heard from her. She asked me to go and check on Danielle and tell her to call home. I went over there after work, thinking I would give her the information and then go see you. But when I got there I knew something was wrong. The dishes were piled high, her bed hadn't been slept in, and when I went into the bathroom I saw two of her prescription drug bottles on the counter completely empty. I looked everywhere for her, and then thought to look out at the water." He let out a deep breath.

"And there she was. I walked to the end of the dock and looked out, thinking I would see her in her kayak or something. Instead I saw her body at the bottom of the lake." He stopped, put his head in his hands. "She came to see me that morning to tell me about the pregnancy, that is one thing I can't get out of my head — she wanted my help and there was nothing I could do."

There was nothing more to say then, we both looked out on the water. I was no longer angry with him, instead I was overwhelmed with grief. I got up from my chair and walked outside and down to the lake. I stood at the dock listening to the waves lapping on the shore. I started to tremble, and then it came, a torrent. I cried uncontrollably, all of my grief just came pouring out. His confession, his engagement, my loss, it was all too much to take. Just hours before I had been thinking about Tom and how happy I was that he was coming to see me. What had happened between now and then to make me feel this way? What was Stuart to me now but a dream that never came true? Stuart was beside me then, he held me and we stood there until my crying jag ended.

"You told me that I made you feel good about yourself. Well, thc truth is, I felt the same way," he said, looking out at the lake. "This place can do strange and wonderful things to people. I'm sorry we never finished where we left off, but I'm not sorry we spent time together. That was the best summer of my life."

It was then I noticed that the mayflies had just hatched and were doing their courtship dance above the water.

PROLOGUE – FIVE YEARS LATER

*From now on, you shall be a small part of every song I sing. —
Myla Seitz*

We were down at the waterfront; I was teaching Mary's ten-year-old son how to skim the flat shale pieces of stone across the lake. Tom was rigging Audrey's old Sunfish with a sail. Karl was ambling towards us, using his cane. At seventy-nine years, the old motorcycle injury was finally taking its toll. I looked past him at the camp, which was now more like a house. It had been renovated with insulation, new roof, siding, an addition for Karl. We could now live here year-round. Tom had a position working as a large animal vet for nearby farms, and I was teaching ecology and aquatic science at a local college.

Karl had an envelope in his hand with my name on the front. He handed it to me.

"I just saw Stuart Lowell. He's in town for a week or so, said his parents are renovating their camp and he had to clean out his room. He found this, and wanted me to give it to you. He had planned to drop it off I guess, but when he saw me at the Marina he ran home to get it."

I opened up the envelope. I had not talked to Stuart in

five years, not since Audrey's death. Inside was a small charm. I remembered it; Laurel had given it to me for my twentieth birthday. It was a silly little charm I used to wear around my neck and never took off. It said: Live Love Laugh. I must have been wearing it that night I spent at Stuart's house watching the moon-rise and fall and somehow it fell off. I remembered thinking I had lost it somewhere and then forgot about it. It was wrapped in a small sheet of paper. There was also a short poem, in Stuart's handwriting:

> *When the sun set, I knew our time together would not last forever and something inside me died. But until that misty morning when the swallows came to life and announced the end of summer, I hadn't realized that the sunrise would predict what the sunset had told us all along. — Author Unknown*

Research on mayflies has shown that some species can molt up to forty times before changing into a winged adult to begin their last fateful flight. I think back now on my twentieth summer and realize that I have shed a lot of skin since then. I have changed and become the person I want to be, and like the mayfly, I am ready to bring forth life. I can feel movement in my womb and I plan to stick around to see how it all turns out.

ACKNOWLEDGEMENTS

I would like to thank the following scientists for sharing their research methods with me over the years: Dale Garner, for his work on the moose populations in Algonquin; Susan Cushman, for her work on aquatic invertebrates; Meghan Brown and her work on the *Mysid* populations in Seneca Lake and John Halfman for his work on water quality parameters for all the lakes. I would also like to thank Bob Werner. He and I trolled Skaneateles Lake the summer of 2013, looking for Eurasian watermilfoil, and he became my sounding board by default. He was the one that alerted me to the fact that bodies will float in warm water, and sink in cold. I would also like to thank David O'Connell for helping me interpret Phaedrus; my editor, Rebecca Kinzie Bastian; and Theseus for his assistance and guidance throughout the editing process.

REFERENCES

Baker, Rannie B. In the Light of Myth: Selection from the World's Myths. Row, Peterson & Co. 1925. Print.

Dickinson, Emily. The soul selects her own society. The Norton Anthology of American Literature. Eighth ed. Vol. B: 1820-1865. Nina Baym and Robert Levine editors. W.W. Norton & Co. 2010. Print.

Garner, Dale. Dissertation on Population Ecology of Moose in Algonquin Provincial Park, Ontario, Canada. State University of New York, College of Environmental Science and Forestry. 1994. Print.

Halpern, Daniel. The Passing. A poem, bibliographic reference unknown.

Klees, Emerson. Person, Places, and Things In the Finger Lakes Region. Friends of the Finger Lakes Publishing. 2000. Print.

Klees, Emerson. Legends and Stories of the Finger Lakes Region. Friends of the Finger Lakes Publishing. 1995. Print.

Krecker, F.H. Phenomena of Orientation Exhibited by Ephemeridae. Biological Bulletin. Vol. 29. 1915. JSTOR.org. Web. Found 06/2013.

Lindbergh, Anne Morrow. Gift from the Sea. Pantheon Books, Inc. 1955. Print.

Morgan, Ann Haven. The Field Book of Ponds and Streams. G.P. Putman's Sons Publishing. 1930. Print.

Pennak, Robert. Freshwater Invertebrates of the United States. The Roland Press Company. 1953. Print.

Plato. Phaedrus. Project Gutenberg: Gutenberg.org. 370 BC. Web. Found 10/2013.

Prather, Hugh. Quote, bibliographic reference unknown.

Rupp, Rebecca. Red Oaks and Black Birches: The Science and Lore of Trees. Garden Way Publishing. 1990. Print.

Schweitzer, Albert. Quote, bibliographic reference unknown.

Seitz (Stauber), Myla. No Title. A poem, bibliographic reference unknown.

Thomson, Tom. Letter to Dr. James MacCallum, 1914. National Gallery of Art Canada. Web. Found 6/2013.

Thoreau, David. The Maine Woods. Houghton Mifflin & Co; Project Gutenberg: Gutenberg.org. 1864. Web. Found 10/2013.

Weeks, John A. Nature's Quiet Conversations. Syracuse University Press. 2006. Print.

NOTES

This is a work of fiction. There are many places mentioned in this book, some are real and some are entirely made up. I will try to decipher what is what to save people time searching the internet for clues.

Canandaigua and Seneca are two of the eleven Finger Lakes. Lake Erie, of course, is one of the five Great Lakes. Roseland Park graced the north end of Canandaigua and the carousel is now at the Destiny USA mall in Syracuse. Bare Hill is a conservation area owned by the State of New York and so is the High Tor Wildlife Preserve. There is a Thendara Restaurant on Canandaigua Lake, and the Owly-Out was a bar I used to frequent with fellow camp counselors on Lake Chateaugay, NY in the Adirondacks. Hobart and William Smith Colleges is in Geneva, NY and has a sixty-five foot research vessel on Seneca Lake, *The William Scandling*. The Colleges also own docks for the sailing team on the shores of Seneca Lake.

Emerson Klees, mentioned as an author on the subject of the Finger Lakes, is from Rochester, NY and has several books published on the history, places and people of the region. The Finger Lakes Land Trust is a non-profit dedicated to open space preservation in the Finger Lakes region. There is a College of Environmental Science and Forestry in Syracuse; I am an alumni. Buffalo State does have a field station on Lake Erie, but it does not have a Vet school. The mayflies were once extirpated on Lake Erie but are making a comeback on the western shore. There is a Mr. Goodbar in Buffalo. Cornell University operates the Ornithology Lab at Sapsucker Woods in Ithaca, NY. There is an Algonquin Provincial Park, an Outpost store and the hand-crafted Algonquin Canoe by the Swift Company. Guelph University owns a research station on Sasajewun

Lake in Algonquin Provincial Park. White pine wood was used as mastheads for the British Navy, and aspens do look like they're talking to each other. There are also documented places where they have cloned themselves (in the West) and are considered one large organism (thanks to Dylan Rothenberg for pointing me to this information while on a trip to the Rockies in Colorado). Tom Thomson is a famous Canadian artist that spent most of his time painting in Algonquin, one of his works is titled *Northern Lights*. There was a bear attack in October, 1991 in Algonquin which led to the tragic death of a couple from Toronto. Like many areas where there are lakes, there have been many deaths in the Finger Lakes due to boating accidents and drownings; I used my knowledge of these incidents as a springboard for my story. There are also documented cases of drug companies being sued for patient death by suicide.

Final Note: I knew someone in High School that had a t-shirt with the saying *Reality is for people that can't handle drugs*. I looked it up on the internet and it seems to be a combination from a quote by Robin P. Williams and Lily Tomlin.

Made in the USA
Charleston, SC
29 May 2014